Emer's Ghost

CATHERINE SEFTON

It was only an old wooden doll with a broken nose that Emer found but she was sure there was something special about it. It certainly did some very undoll-like things like crying real tears in the middle of the night, and it was definitely the doll that led Emer to the ghost.

That much was clear, but what did the ghost *want*? Emer is determined to find out. But when she gets on the right track it seems as though there may be real danger ahead before she can solve the mystery . . . .

CATHERINE SEFTON

Emer's Ghost

Mammoth

First published in Great Britain 1981
by Hamish Hamilton Children's Books
Magnet paperback edition first published 1983
Reissued 1990 by Mammoth
an imprint of Mandarin Paperbacks
Michelin House, 81 Fulham Road, London SW3 6RB
Reprinted 1991

Mandarin is an imprint of the Octopus Publishing Group

ISBN 0 7497 0690 2

A CIP catalogue record for this title
is available from the British Library

Printed and bound in Great Britain by
BPCC Hazell Books
Aylesbury, Bucks, England
Member of BPCC Ltd.

for
Kathleen with the happy face

Chapter One

"Emer! Emer McAnna!"

The sharp note of annoyance in Sister Consuelo's voice brought me back to reality. I had been miles away, thinking about our gull.

"Are you with us today, Emer?" asked Sister Consuelo, sourly. "We are supposed to be Viking Raiders laying waste the Christian Communities on the shores of Carlingford Lough. May we rely upon your sturdy long sword for assistance?"

There was a giggle behind me, which was Rosa Davis and Sally Doran enjoying themselves at my expense. They had nothing to giggle about. They were draped together in a grey blanket being a round tower.

Sister Consuelo's icy glare silenced them. We are all scared of Sister Consuelo and her glares, although she isn't the worst of the nuns. She is Art and Drama as well as our form teacher, so I suppose she must be a progressive nun.

"Emer?" she said.

"Yes, Sister," I said.

"Yes, Sister, *what*, Emer?"

"Yes, Sister, I'll remember that I am supposed to be a Viking." How could I forget, walking around with a string wig on my head and a long sword in my hand?

Off she went on her explanation of What-We-Must-Do-When-The-Bishop-Comes. I made a face at the Round Tower, and Rosa and Sally made some most unroundtower-like faces back. My sister Breige, who was being a Christian, tried to look as if we weren't happening to her. Breige put her holy face on, and sat there lapping it all up. There was a lot to lap, because the nuns are all nuts about bishops.

Sister knew that I wasn't paying attention and, when the bell went, she called me back.

"Emer, will you wait behind the others a moment, please?" she said, as I gathered my bag and started for the door.

Then she left me standing there clutching my bag and long sword, while everybody else got out and headed for the cloakroom, discarding hundreds of years of the History of Bloody Headland as they ran, a Bishop's Pageant in retreat. I stole a look at the clock over Sister Consuelo's desk, knowing that I couldn't spend much more time standing there, or I would miss the bus.

Breige and I are the only two from our house at the Convent Girls, for Peter is a boy, and Kathleen is already at the Secondary in Tullyvannet. Going to the Convent School on the bus means that we are often late home, for the bus goes all around the country before it gets to the Bloody Headland, and then we have to get off and make our way across to our own house at Craggy Man. We are always last into our house, which does not matter much when my Mother is at home, but causes trouble on a Friday when Kathleen is doing the tea. She has a lot of homework, because of her exams, and she likes to get the tea over quickly.

3

"Sister?" I said, in case she had forgotten about me.

"Well, Emer?" She put her books flat on the desk with a little bang, as if she wished that she was banging my head.

"Sister, my bus!"

"There is no good your coming miles on your bus, if you are not going to pay any attention to what goes on when you get here, is there, Emer?"

"No, Sister."

"It isn't just me, is it, Emer? Sister Catherine, Sister Bonaventure. . ." She waited, as if she expected me to say something. I wasn't surprised that Sister Catherine was complaining, because she is Music, but I bet she was making up Sister Bonaventure. It isn't my fault that school is so boring.

"This is a last warning, Emer. Do you understand me?"

"Yes, Sister."

"Don't 'Yes, Sister' me, Emer, unless you mean to do something about it. And stop hopping around like that! You are a clever child, if you

4

would only put your mind to it and concentrate on what you are supposed to be doing. You have too many notions in that head of yours, Emer! Your behaviour is not good enough."

"No, Sister."

"Indeed, '*no*' Emer!" she said, snapping her books together as she rose from her seat. She isn't that bad, it is just that I don't like her. "That is all for now, Emer. Cut and run and you will make your bus. Have a nice week-end, and think about what I've said. I don't want to have to give you a note for your mother."

"*No*, Sister!" I said, horrified.

"But that won't be necessary, will it?" she said. "Off you go."

"Yes, Sister. Thank you, Sister," I said.

I was halfway down the corridor when she called after me from the classroom doorway, and I had to come trailing all the way back.

"Emer, dear. You haven't put your sword away in the prop cupboard, have you? If you leave it there, poor Sister Bonaventure will break her neck over it."

"Yes, Sister," I said, retrieving my sword from the floor. Sister Bonaventure is always tripping over things. She is a very big nun, and she sometimes doesn't look where she is going. She says things jump out on her. I bounced across the room and chucked my sword into the cupboard on top of the burning torches and Cromwellian armour we needed for the Pageant.

"I think you should take your wig off before you go out, Emer," Sister Consuelo said. I looked at her face to see if she was laughing at me, but she never moved a muscle. I was still scared by the threat that she would give me a note for my Mother.

My Mother has had enough trouble, without getting notes about me from school. I just won't give it to her, I thought, but I knew that I would have to. The nuns are great ones for following up things like that and in a small school like ours nobody gets away with anything. Kathleen gets away with murder at Tullyvannet Secondary, but we are not so lucky.

I stuffed my wig into my bag, and banged the

prop cupboard door shut.

"Emer!" Sister Consuelo exclaimed, sounding pained. Visions of the note to my mother competed with visions of me missing the bus.

"Sister . . . my *bus*! *Sister*!"

"Off you go," she said.

Off I went like Concorde, heading for Mayo Bridge bus stop with my bag under one arm and my anorak under the other, my Viking jerkin flapping around my knees.

"Hi! Here comes the Craggy Man Canute!" Rosa Davis sang out when she saw me coming, so I stood on her toe, hard, as we were clambering onto the bus. I was almost the last one there, and I had to squeeze on with the standers. Breige was already perched in her favourite nest, third from the back by the window, with her nose in a book. She hadn't kept me a place, which was very nice of her I don't think.

There was no hope of a seat until after Plumbridge and Killoo when the Mineworker's Mountain children got off. By the time I got in beside Breige the bus was almost empty.

7

"I don't see why I have to be a Viking," I said. They had been calling me the Craggy Man Canute ever since Rosa thought of it, and I was fed up.

"You are always banging about the place and causing riots," said Breige, putting down her book. "I think that you are rather Viking-like, myself. And you know what Mrs. Thomason said when we were doing life-saving last summer. She said you were 'a holy terror'. I think she was right."

"Oh," I said. It wouldn't have been so bad if they'd let me be a Cromwellian, burning down the Burnt Church, because the Cromwellians didn't have string wigs. It was the string wig that really annoyed me.

"If you are really worried about it, I'll ask Sister if we can swop," Breige offered. "I could be a Viking killing people and you could be a Christian hiding your Holy Relics in a souter-whatever-it-is."

"Souterrain," I said. "But I don't think I want to be a Christian, either. I don't fancy looking soulful and running around wrapped up in a blanket.''

"Monks," said Breige, reprovingly. "We are supposed to be monks. The Vikings come roaring up the Lough to lay waste our settlements and we hide all our treasures in the souter-whatever-it-is and get up into our Round Tower and drop things on them."

"I don't think the monks did drop things on Vikings," I said. "Except other monks, probably. They might have tipped an odd monk they didn't like out of the Round Tower at Viking-time, I suppose."

"Let me remind you that I am the monk on this bus," said Breige. "You are a mere Viking, so shut up!" And she went back to her book.

The bus turned at the Bloody Headland Cottages which are the end of the line for it. We hopped off with the papers for Hogan's tin shop which were done up in their yellow wrapper as usual. We usually leave the papers in the hedge in Hogan's Lane, and then cut across the disused airfield to our own place. There are just two houses lived in around the airfield, ours and Hogan's shop, which is why it is not a very big shop! That is not the real reason, which is that Hector Hogan does most of the shop business from his van going round the countryside, and the tin shop is just his house and a store, and not a real shop at all, although he does sell things from it if you can catch him there.

We came down the lane toward the bit of hedge where we usually drop the papers, but we didn't get a chance to drop them.

"Look!" I said.

Hector's van was in the ditch, with the windscreen smashed in around his bananas, and half his groceries spread out across the lane.

"Did you ever see so many eggs?" Breige said.

"Come on!" I pulled her arm, and we took off down the lane toward the accident. The van had crashed into the stone ditch, just beyond the path to the ruined houses on the edge of our airfield. The front end was hanging into the Coastguard's field, and Willie Annett and Sam Smyth were in the field with Mikey Samuel, clearing away the rocks.

Hector was sitting in the ditch, looking tired and cross.

"Are you all right, Hector? Did you have an accident?" Breige said.

She is a braver soul than I am! I would not have spoken to Hector. Once she had spoken, he was off like a greyhound.

"Accident!" he gurgled. "Did I just have an accident, wee McAnna! Amn't I drove into the ditch and the front of me van stove in and me stock in pieces and did-I-have-an-accident! Did I just! Him and his bicycle! I should have drove over him for trespassing! Him and his bicycle and '*Did-you-not-see-me-coming*?' What right has that old blaggard or any other Bannon in my lane? What right, I'd like to know? I'll see him coming another time. I'll see him in another place if he won't keep off my land. I'll . . ."

I ducked down into the Coastguard's field, out of the way. Poor Breige was left standing with her mouth wide open, in front of Hector, who was waving his arms about, and getting redder and

11

redder in the face.

"*Him and his bicycle!*" came floating over the hedge.

"Was it Baldie he ran into?" I asked Mikey Samuel, anxiously. I was afraid that Baldie might have been hurt. He is as strong as a horse, but he is an old man. He's a great friend of mine, and helps with my hens.

"It would take more than Hector Hogan's van to fell that tree trunk! A knock on the head and a bit of a buffet when he landed in the ditch will do him no harm, and maybe knock a bit of sense into him."

"He is a very sensible person," I said, for I wasn't going to stand for anybody running Baldie down behind his back. Mikey and the others all think that Baldie is mad, but he is not. He just doesn't speak to grown-ups much, except his mother, but he speaks to us.

"Aye, well," said Mikey, with a grin. "You should see Baldie in a full moon! According to Hector he came out of the hedge with his bike, and damn near chucked it at the van! Hector swerved into the ditch, and now the shop-van is busted, and Hector is after Baldie Bannon's blood.

"Oh," I said.

"Baldie is away now in Sister Bonaventure's car, for she was down at the diggings by the Burnt Church when she heard the bang. He is safer at home in the cottage with his mother. Hector would have had him by the throat."

I thought about it.

"Baldie was wheeling his bicycle down the lane, and Hector ran right into him," I said.

"Ould eejit on his pedal bike!" Hector erupted over the top of the ditch, dropping down into the field behind us.

"Did you not see him walking along, Hector?" I said, but luckily he didn't hear me.

"Keep your mouth shut!" Mikey hissed, and he grabbed his crowbar and set to work at the front of the shop van.

I clambered back through the hole in the ditch to join Breige.

"Look at that," she said, prodding with the side

13

of her foot at the dirty object that lay among the broken eggs in the lane. She made a face at me.

"Baldie's hat," I said, retrieving it.

"I've never seen him without his hat," Breige said.

"He must have been in a bad way to go home without it," I said.

"You know what Hector was doing?" Breige asked, turning away from the van. "He was bumping down that lane at full speed with his head in the clouds, that's what! It is a wonder he hasn't killed somebody before now. How did he ever pass the driving test?"

"I doubt if he ever sat it," I said, fingering the brim of the hat.

"This will mean more bad blood between the Hogans and the Bannons," Breige said.

She was right. There is a long standing feud between Hector Hogan and the Bannons because Hector had bought the Bannons' land, the bit that was taken from them by the Government to make the airfield at Craggy Man. When the war was over the Government didn't need the airfield any more, and they sold most if it to Hector, who paid them a fair price for it. The trouble was that he did not pay anything to the Bannons, who had got next to nothing for it when the Government took it from them. Baldie and his Mother say that the land is still theirs by right, and the old houses on it, which are no more than ruins now. Hector won't agree to that at all, because he bought it fair and square from the Government and paid good money. It is stupid, if you ask me, but that is the way it is. There is nothing worse in our country than a row about land.

"I tell you what," Breige said. "After we have had some tea and seen to our gull we will walk down to Bannon's cottage and give Baldie back his hat, will we?"

And that is what we did.

I stuck Baldie's hat in my anorak pocket and we went home for our tea. The idea of going down to Baldie Bannon's cottage seemed of no account at the time, but it was from that cold evening expedition that all my trouble started.

Chapter Two

"Are we going to Bannons' or not?" I asked Breige, when we had finished our tea.

"In a minute," said Breige, who had curled up in my Father's chair by the range, with her book.

"Where are you two going?" said Kathleen, coming into the kitchen. She pushed her hair out of her eyes, and settled her specs back on her nose. It is a pity about the specs. They would not look so bad if she could keep them on her nose.

"We want to see if Baldie is all right, after the accident," I said. "We rescued his hat."

"Baldie Bannon?"

"Yes."

"He's nuts," Kathleen said.

"He's not," said Breige.

"Nobody is going anywhere out of this house

16

until the dishes are done," said Kathleen, going over to poke the range. When she straightened up from doing it her face was as shiny as the sun. She had her stripey jersey on, one with a hole in the sleeve. She saw me looking at it.

"What are you gawping at?" she asked.

"You'll not go to see your student with that on!" I said.

"I don't know what you're talking about," she answered.

"Yes you do," said Breige, looking up from her book. "Your boy friend with the shovel."

"I don't like people poking around our places with their strings and ropes and shovels," said Peter, taking the saw from the wall. Peter's job is the driftwood. I do the hens. Kathleen and Breige do the house. . . at least, Breige does her bit when Kathleen can catch her. Our Breige is a wily bird.

"He is an archaeologist," Breige said. "His job is poking around old places. Archaeologists spend all their time doing it."

"Not *all* their time," I said, with a meaningful look at Kathleen.

"Emer!" she said. "Dishes!"

I went to do the dishes. It was really Breige's job, but I had a deal going with Breige, doing the dishes in exchange for using her bicycle. "He is not a proper archaeologist, anyway," I said, from the scullery. "None of them are, except Professor Meredith. Kathleen's man is only a student."

"Shut up, Emer," said Kathleen.

"Yes, Emer, just shut up for five minutes and do those dishes, will you?" said Breige. "I am trying to read!" And she grinned at me.

"Dishwasher general, that's me!" I said, but I went on with the job, wishing the scullery hadn't got a stone floor. My great-grandfather built our house out of solid Mourne Rock. It is a great house, but I don't think he was ever in the scullery! The scullery has a stone floor which is very cold. The whole place could do with central heating, but my great-grandfather installed central draughts instead, and they are with us to this day.

I get on well with my family, most times, despite having a grudge against my great-grand-

18

father. I get on best of all with Breige, and next Peter, and I suppose I don't get on so well with Kathleen because she is so much older than the rest of us, and always in a rush with things to do. Since my Father died my Mother has been going into Tullyvannet to work at "Mourne View" Hotel and Kathleen has a lot of helping to do as well as all her homework and worrying about her exams. I would not like to be Kathleen, and I feel especially sorry for her about the specs.

I spent a moment or two scrounging bacon rinds to put with the hen meal for our gull. We found our gull on the beach, with a broken wing. Baldie Bannon said it would starve, and if it didn't starve the foxes would get it. So we hid it in Bannon's hidey hole at the old houses, and we brought it food specially, and so far it was still eating and the foxes hadn't got it. We were hoping that it would be all right, if it didn't pull off the splint that Baldie had made for its wing. I put the bacon rinds in a paper bag, and then I came out of the scullery and hung the drying cloth on the range bar.

"Right, Breige, are you ready?"

"You will both wrap up well before you go over that doorstep," said Kathleen. "It's a good walk across the fields to the Bloody Headland houses, and there is a nip in the air."

Which is how we came to be all dolled up like Eskimos, going for a brisk evening walk across the back fields. Spring or not there was still some snow high up on the Mournes, which are the big mountains that stretch down to the shore. I felt a bit daft, and hoped that nobody would see us, all done up in scarves and gloves and hats.

"The men are still working at the shop van," Breige said, as we came up to the ruins of the old houses. "I think we should give our gull the miss, for we don't want them to find Baldie's hidey hole. We can feed it on the way back."

"What are they doing?" I asked, a bit puzzled. From what we could see over the hedges to the lane, they seemed to be moving stuff in Mikey Samuel's trailer.

"From the look of them, they'll be over this way in a minute," Breige said. "Come on, we can find out what they're up to on the way back."

So Breige didn't want Mikey to see her dressed up as an Eskimo either! I followed her through the airfield fence and we turned down toward the Bloody Headland, following the lane toward the row of tiny cottages and the gaunt shape of the Burnt Church. Some of Cromwell's marauders burned it when they didn't find what they expected, and they killed most of the local people at the same time, which is how the place got its name; the Bloody Headland.

"Have you the hat?" Breige said, when we got down as far as Bannons' cottage.

I took it out of my pocket and poked it straight, as best I could, then I nodded and she knocked.

Baldie answered the door to us. He had a towel on his head.

"Just washing the hair," he said.

"We came to bring back your hat," Breige said, grinning all over her face. I held it out, and he snatched it out of my hand and retreated back into the cottage. When he emerged a moment later, the hat was on his head.

"We wanted to be sure you weren't hurt," I said, politely.

"I'm not," he said, giving us a cute look. I think he was challenging us to say something about his hair, or the lack of it.

"Is your bike bust, Mr. Bannon?" Breige asked.

"Not too bad, not too bad," he said. I couldn't keep the grin off my face, looking at the hat on his head and the towel in his hand.

"We. . . we thought we'd call and see. In case you were ill, and your Mother needed anything," I said.

"We wasted our time," Breige grumbled, when we had made our escape. "The world is right, and we are wrong. He is cracked, and no mistake!"

"He is not," I said. "He is just no kind of a conversationalist. And he did give us the fish."

Baldie had given us fish for our gull. Breige put up her nose at it, but I was glad enough. I couldn't help but worry about our gull, for he didn't seem keen on the hen meal and bacon rind.

"Just so long as you carry it," Breige said.

We turned down Hogan's Lane. Hector's shop van was back on four wheels, standing deserted by the ditch.

"It still has groceries in it," said Breige, in a puzzled voice.

"What were they moving in the trailer?" I asked.

"Search me!" said Breige.

We stood looking at the break in the old ditch, where the van had gone into it.

"Trust Hector to go around wrecking the place!" I grumbled. I clambered down into the Coastguard's field, but as I did so part of the ditch gave way under me, and I tobogganed down, with rubble all about me.

"Are you all right, Emer?" Breige said, clambering after me.

I was, and I wasn't.

I had no bones broken, but I had a funny feeling. I can't really describe it. It was as if my heart had stopped, just for a moment.

"I'm. . . I'm. . . would you look at that!" I said, reaching out my hand into the fallen rubble that

23

I'd disturbed.

"What?" said Breige, scrambling down beside me.

"Wait till I get at it!" I said, and I tugged at the dirty thing in the rubble and it came away in my hand.

It was a small figure, a doll, no size at all, with a face battered by time and rock.

"What is it? What've you got?" Breige said, taking it from me.

"It's a doll," I said, slowly.

"It's all mucky!" she said, dropping the doll. "Chuck it away!"

I looked at it, and my funny feeling grew. The battered little figure had been hidden safe in the ditch, till Hector's van wrecked the place. Lying there for years and years. . . I wasn't going to chuck it away.

"Emer!" Breige said. "You're pale as a ghost! Did somebody walk on your grave?"

I paid no attention to her. I picked the doll up, and rubbed the dirt off it with my finger, tracing the stub of the little broken face.

"You're not having that thing in our room!" Breige said.

"I'll have it if I want it!" I said.

"Not in my half, okay?"

"Okay!" I said.

Then I stuck the doll in the pocket of my anorak and took her home.

If I'd known then what I know now I would have. . . . I don't know. Maybe I'd have done just the same thing.

Chapter Three

It was midnight.

I had been asleep and something had wakened me up, I didn't know what. I could see that it was midnight by looking at Breige's clock on the mantelpiece. It was seven minutes past midnight, to be exact.

There was a very soft pattering noise, which puzzled me, but only for a moment, then I knew what it was.

Snow.

Snow in April. Our room is right up against the roof. The soft sound of the snow on the tiles was like someone whispering.

I sat up in bed and looked at the window. It is a small square window, set in the thick stone wall of our house, with a wide window ledge.

Kathleen made us blue curtains for it, that match our bedspreads. Breige had pulled the curtains back because she likes the light first thing in the morning, and the view across the Lough. I could see the distant lights of the houses on the other side of the Lough, and just about make out the dark shape of the Burnt Church on our side.

The wooden doll was standing on the window ledge, where I had left her. The window is in my half of the room. Breige has the mantelpiece and the top of the wardrobe for putting things on and we have our Life Saving Certificates on the wall to make a half-way mark.

I felt uneasy.

I lay in bed watching the wooden doll watching me.

I knew that she was just a doll, of course. She was only three or four inches high, rounded, like a small milk bottle, with her chubby arms . . . or what was left of them . . . gathered across her chest. She had weathered badly. All the sharp bits of her, like her ears and nose, were worn almost smooth, and there was a bad crack across her back, but she was still a doll.

The thing was, she kept looking at me.

It *had* to be imagination. I knew that. But *knowing* it, I couldn't rob myself of the feeling that the wooden doll was watching me.

"Right!" I thought, and I poked under my pillow for my torch, which I always keep there in case the lights go off. Our electricity is always going off, because of the wind blowing down the power lines along the coast. I didn't want to use the bedside lamp on the table between the two beds in case the light would waken Breige, and she would think that I had gone out of my tiny mind.

I switched on the torch, determined to stop the doll nonsense once and for all, and got out of bed. I walked over to the window, and picked up the doll, to have a closer look at her.

She was hard and cold in my hand. There was no intelligence there, nothing to be afraid of.

"There," I said, out loud, holding her in front of me, with her broken face close up to mine.

I touched her head, ran my finger down the stump of her nose, and then I had one of the worst shocks of my whole life.

When I drew my finger back from her face it was damp.

The wooden doll had been crying.

Chapter Four

"Condensation!" said Breige, gleefully.

"Shut up," I said, growing red.

"Wakened me up in the middle of the night," Breige said. " 'Oh look, Breige, my dolly is crying!' "

"I did not!"

"You did."

"I didn't mean to."

"You let a howl out of you that would have wakened the dead," said Breige.

"We learned about condensation in P.3 Class," said Peter.

"I'm glad you learn something in school," said Breige.

"I know all about condensation," I said, blushing even more. "I didn't think of it, that's all."

"Didums think ums dolly was crying?" said Peter. "Dere, dere, den, didums?"

"Shut up!" I shouted, and my shout brought Kathleen out of the scullery, potato knife in hand.

"Stop that fighting, or you'll wake Mammy," she said. "Don't you know it is Saturday? She needs her long lie in. What is the matter with you lot this morning anyway?"

"Emer got a scare last night," Breige said. "She thought her icky wicky wee dolly wolly was crying real tears and she made a whole fuss and wakened me up to tell me about it. And it was only condensation! The window was dripping with it, and so was the old wooden doll."

"Honestly, you are a fool, Emer." Kathleen said. "But that is enough. Joke over, okay?"

I was glad to get out of the room, I can tell you. I went up to our room and straight over to the window where the doll was. I had a good mind to get rid of her. . . but that would only have pleased Breige, and given her another laugh at me. I wasn't going to give her the satisfaction of saying I was so scared that I'd had to get rid of the doll. Silly anyway! *Condensation*!

I went down the back stairs to avoid Breige and out into the back, where I collected the eggs for Hector in my egg basin, then clambered up on the airfield wall, ready to take the short cut over by the old houses to Hector's. I was standing on the top of the wall when I saw someone nosing about on our airfield.

The airfield is a very big flat place with the gaunt frame of the control tower still sticking up, and the floors of the Nissen huts still there, but very little else. The runways have run away to nothing amongst the weeds. There are rolls of barbed wire looped out across what is left of them to stop the people from Ballagh racing their cars and motorbikes, and a few dug-outs that Hector uses for his creels. The snow had left the airfield frozen white and there was still a swirl of it in the air.

It was a man. I thought it might be Kathleen's student, but as he came closer I could see that it was not. It was Sergeant Benny Cunningham, of the R.U.C.. R.U.C. stands for "Royal Ulster Constabulary" which is what we call our police force in Northern Ireland.

I stopped and stood where I was, waiting to see what he would do. I had my heart in my mouth for Mikey Samuel had warned me what would happen if anyone found out about Hector selling my eggs in his van shop. My eggs are illegal since we got into the Common Market and Hector should not be selling them, but he does.

I slipped down off the wall into the cold grass, bringing my basin of eggs with me. If he saw my eggs I would be arrested and if I moved they would rattle in the basin and he might think I was a murderer there to shoot him, and maybe he would shoot me instead.

It felt odd to be hiding on the airfield, because it is more or less our backfield, although it belongs to Hector. We have always played there, and we go across it every day to his tin shop, or to get down to the cottages at the Bloody Headland. I knew Hector wouldn't mind me, but I wasn't taking any chances with a policeman. I stayed crouched down beside the wall, completely hidden in the snowy grass.

The Sergeant went on across the airfield, toward the gap at Hogan's, hitching at his bullet proof vest. I suppose if I was a policeman in Northern Ireland I would be fretful too, in case somebody would shoot me, especially on a wild lonely place like our airfield.

I let him go, but when he had gone I hid my eggs double quick and then I ran across the field and down the path by Bannons' old houses and the hidey hole, out into Hogan's lane. It was the long way round, but I meant to go on up the lane and in round the back of the tin shop to see what was going on.

It isn't everyday your neighbours get arrested!

Of course, Sergeant Benny Cunningham was there ahead of me, and he was standing at Hector's door, arguing. He wasn't the only one either. There were other men in uniforms there, but they were not policemen.

"Where are they?" I heard Hector say, with a

smile on his face. I have never known that smile of Hector's to mean good for anyone but Hector Hogan.

"By all accounts they were all over your lane yesterday, when you went into the ditch," said Sergeant Benny.

Hector said something that I couldn't catch, but the Sergeant didn't look pleased. One of the other uniformed men called him aside. They talked for a moment or two, and then he went back to Hector.

"It looks as if you are off the hook this time," he said. "But I'll be back about the van, Hector, never fear."

"Mr. Hogan to you," said Hector, and he slammed the shop door in the policeman's face.

The Sergeant had a conversation with the other men, and then they went off in their van, whilst he set off along the beach toward the Bloody Headland cottages, his feet sinking in the sand.

He was no sooner out of the way than Hector emerged from the shop, and gave a whistle. Mikey Samuel came skidding and sliding down the sand bank at the side.

"Gone!" Hector said.

"And not an egg about the place!" said Mikey. "That was a grand night's work and no mistake."

I jumped over the wall, making the two of them start. When Hector saw it was only me, he laughed.

"Wee McAnna, is it?" he said.

"I was bringing the eggs," I said.

"Eggs!" said Mikey, as though it was the greatest joke in the world, and they both started laughing.

"You may keep away from me with eggs for a while, child," said Hector.

"Was it. . . was it *my* eggs they were arresting you for?" I asked. "It *wasn't*! I don't believe it!"

Hector stopped laughing.

"It was," he said.

Then he winked at Mikey.

"In soul it was," said Mikey. "You have this man in terrible trouble with the police."

"Terrible," said Hector.

I didn't know what to make of them. I had seen the policeman with my own eyes, but I couldn't

36

believe there would be all that fuss over my eggs.

"This child here, Mikey," said Hector. "She is not a bad child, but she will not learn the regulations. According to the law, there are big eggs from big hens, wee eggs from wee hens, and medium sized eggs from medium sized hens. But McAnna's hens ... you never know what size will pop out of them next."

"You are pulling my leg," I said, feeling sore.

"Indeed we are not," said Mikey. "That is the way the law is, since we joined the Common Market."

And they both had another good laugh at my expense.

"You may go home and give your hens a good talking to," said Hector.

Off I went, for I wasn't standing there to let them laugh at me.

I went back by the lane, and up to the old houses, to have a look at our gull. The hidey hole is round the back, hidden away where no-one would see it who did not know it was there. It was Baldie who showed it to us, for he used to use it for his things, before the Bannons were moved off the airfield ground by the Government, in the war. It is an old stone place, but once you slip inside the narrow entrance it is not so bad, for there is a small chamber that is almost a passage, where Baldie still keeps some old things of his, and where he said our gull would be safe. So it was in there that we had put him.

I had my torch in my anorak pocket, and I flashed it on, as soon as I was through the entrance and able to stand up.

No gull!

There was his box, and a few scattered bits of the fish we had brought him, but no gull. He wasn't well enough to fly, so he couldn't have gone that way. The foxes. . . but there were no feathers. I have seen enough of foxes to know they do not do a clean job.

I flashed my torch round. . . and then I heard something move. I went over by Baldie's boxes, and pulled one aside. There was our gull, hidden away. It looked at me, but it did not try to move.

A gull is its own thing, a wild thing. It does not

take to you the way a hen will, or a robin on the wall. A gull will put up with you, but it has its own dignity, and that goes even for a gull with a broken wing.

"What chased you in there, gull?" I said, but I did not try to touch it. Instead I got down the meal I had left in Baldie's boxes, and mingled it in with the bacon rind and bread I had brought, and put them where the gull could get them.

"There you are now. That's your breakfast," I said.

The gull didn't look at me.

"How's your wing?" I said. It had the broken wing side away from me. I bent down, and reached round the side of the box. It snuggled forward, away from my hand, and turned its head back at me, opening and shutting its beak.

"All right," I said, "don't put yourself out!" But I was cheerful enough. Our gull was looking livelier than it had yet been. It was a good sign that it had managed to get out of the bed we had made for it and find its own place, hidden among the boxes.

I wondered if something had disturbed it, and I was still wondering when I saw the footprint.

My first thought was that it was Baldie's, because he wears big boots, and the footprint was certainly not a child's. But Baldie had nails in his boots, and this print had a swirly pattern. So that was why our gull had hidden itself away! Strangers!

I got out of the hidey hole and into the daylight as quickly as I could, anxious to get hold of Breige, and see what we should do. The hidey hole was our secret place, and nobody else but Baldie was supposed to know about it. Now ... well, somebody had been inside.

Home, I thought, and I turned to run down toward the houses, and saw that someone had been watching me.

My first thought was that it was Kathleen, but then I knew that it was not.

She was standing very still, and she was very small, and she wasn't like Kathleen at all.

She was grey against the white of the snow, almost colourless, and I could see right through her, to the wall of the back lane.

"Oh, dear God!" I said.

I stood within feet of her, looking at her. Her eyes were closed, and her hands were by her sides. She had long hair that ran down to her waist, and a rough cloth garment like a cloak that fastened round her neck.

I could see the snow falling through her as if she wasn't there.

But she *was* there.

She came drifting slowly toward me up the slope from the houses, as if she was being blown by the wind, but there was no wind.

"Go. Go away!" I said.

It was the only thing I could think of to say, I was so scared.

She stopped.

She opened her eyes, like somebody wakened out of sleep, then she moved her arms out toward me, as though I had something that she wanted, and then she faded away.

One minute the tiny grey figure was blocking my path, and the next she was gone.

Chapter Five

"Emer's seen a ghost on our airfield!" Peter shouted out, hopping round the back of the arm-chair, out of my reach.

"And it went bugga-wugga-bugga-wugga-woo!" Breige sang out gleefully.

"It isn't funny," I said.

"Yes it is," said Peter. "It is very, very funny."

"Bugga-wugga-wooooooo!" said Breige. Then she pulled her jersey up over her head and wag-gled her arms about. "I am the Ghost of Bannons' old houses come to claim my ghostly inheritance! Bugga-wugga-woo!"

"Shut up," I said.

"You are a daft egg, Emer," said Kathleen.

"Ghosts!"

"And crying dolls," said Peter. "Don't forget

the cry baby dolly."

I stirred uneasily.

"Bugga-wugga-woo!" Breige sang out, staggering round the sofa. "Bugga-wugga-wugga-wugga-wooo!"

She was in mid "woo" when Mammy walked in.

"Bugga-wugga-woo! Emer is nutty as a fruit cake!" Breige shouted, dancing around with her jersey pulled over her head. She couldn't see Mammy, who was standing behind her in the doorway.

"Breige," said Kathleen, in her warning voice.

"I am the Fruit Cake of the Haunted Houses!" Breige shouted, jumping up on the sofa and wagging her arms about, completely carried away in her ghost imitation.

"*Breige*," said Mammy.

"Woooo. . .ooh!" said Breige.

Her face popped out of the neck of her jersey, looking startled, and she sat down on the sofa, quickly.

"Well?" Mammy said.

43

"They were just carrying on," Kathleen said.

"And Emer saw a ghost over at the old houses," said Peter. "On the airfield. Bannons'."

"And it went bugga-woo!" said Breige, unable to resist making her joke again.

"If I see you hopping around on the furniture like that you'll go bugga woo!" said Mammy, grimly. "I've never heard so much shouting and noise in all my born days. What a carry-on! You should be ashamed of yourselves. Kathleen, you are supposed to have more wit than the others. Could you not at least have stopped them from dancing on the furniture? I'm surprised at the lot of you."

"It's Emer," Breige said. "Being a Viking has gone to her head. She had. . ."

"That's enough about Emer, Breige," said Kathleen. "Sorry, Mammy."

My mother went across the room and sat down in her chair. She was in her dressing-gown, and for the first time I realised how tired she was looking. It is working at the "Mourne View" hotel that tires her out, for she has to bicycle home from Tullyvannet in the middle of the night, and sometimes it is one or two o'clock before she gets in. I was sorry we had all been making so much noise.

"I'll make you a cup of tea," Kathleen volunteered, trying to make things up to her.

"I'm sorry if we wakened you up," Breige said. Mammy looked so pale and tired that even she had noticed.

"It is a bit late to be sorry," Kathleen said. "Go on, clear off and do something useful."

"Well, we are sorry anyway, aren't we?" Breige said, and Peter and I nodded.

"Look at your jersey, Breige!" Mammy said. "You have it all pulled out of shape. Honestly, *Breige*!"

"I'll go and change it," Breige said, and she nipped out of the room as quickly as she could, more to get out of Mammy's way than anything else.

"I don't know what good changing it is going to do," Kathleen grumbled, going into the kitchen. Peter trailed after her.

45

"Well, Emer?" my mother said.

I didn't say anything. How could I? She was so tired and I didn't want to bother her and anyway nobody would believe me, not even Mammy.

"You look very pale, child, are you all right?"

"Yes."

"And what is all this about seeing things?"

"Nothing."

"Nothing?"

"I was. . . I was just making it up for a laugh," I said, wishing that I had been.

"It seems a silly thing for you to be making up," she said, disapprovingly.

"I won't do it again," I said, and escaped from the room.

I went up to our bedroom. Breige had put the wooden doll behind the curtain. I took it out again, and placed it on the middle of the window ledge. Then I turned it round so that it could look out over the airfield at the Burnt Church and the Lough, and not at me.

Chapter Six

"Pax?" Breige said.

"Only if you promise to shut up," I said.

"I won't say so much as a bugga-woo!"

We had finished our jobs and were looking for something to do.

"What'll we do?" I asked.

"Let's creep after Kathleen," Breige said.

"Why?" I said. Kathleen had gone off down to the Bloody Headland to see about getting oil from the oil man, who doesn't usually come to us unless word is left with the Smyths at the cottages.

"You'll see why," said Breige.

"Oh, I nearly forgot!" I exclaimed, and I told her about the footprint in the hidey hole. "So somebody else knows it is there as well as us,

47

Breige. What should we do?"

"Nothing," said Breige.

"I know, but. . ."

"You like it being ours. But it isn't really ours. It belongs to Hector Hogan, at least it is on his land, and if it doesn't belong to Hector it belongs to Baldie Bannon, and it certainly doesn't belong to us. We can't put up 'Trespassers Keep Out' signs can we?"

"They might harm our gull," I said.

"And they might not," she said.

She wasn't prepared to do anything, and I hadn't much idea of what I wanted done myself. The only thing I could do was to keep a closer watch on the hidey hole and . . . well, that brought up problems.

I hadn't imagined it. I had seen a ghost. I believed that, because I had to, it had happened to me. I knew what I'd seen, even if nobody else did. I'd seen the figure of a girl, drifting toward me. . . moving, but the actual figure absolutely still. . . much younger than me, quite tiny really, and I knew she was a ghost because I had seen the snow falling through her.

It *couldn't* have happened.

But it had.

I had seen her.

Seen a Ghost.

I'd read about ghosts in books; people are always seeing ghosts in books. But you don't expect to see one in real life. Well, I had. It was scaring, but not as scaring as I'd thought it would be. I couldn't be frightened of that tiny girl with the outstretched arms and the plaintive eyes and the long flowing hair She didn't mean me any harm, I was convinced of that. *What*, then. . .? Biggest question of all.

Why me?

We ran across the airfield, and nipped over the wall. The snow had stopped and the cold sunlight glistened on the water of Carlingford Lough. We came across the Coastguard's field, and down onto the beach, making our way toward the Bloody Headland.

"There," Breige said, pointing to the field

beyond the Burnt Church where the archaeological dig was going on. "I told you Kathleen didn't leave her glasses behind for nothing."

Kathleen was down at the edge of the old grave yard, leaning on the wall, talking to her student, who was in the field. He was showing her something on the ground, where they had it marked out with ropes and stakes. He was showing something to her, but I doubt if she could see much, without her glasses.

"So much for going for the oil!" Breige said.

"Yes, well, so what?" I said, a little annoyed, for it didn't seem fair to be spying on Kathleen.

"We will have a good joke on her about it when she gets home," Breige said, with satisfaction.

"You will, if you want," I said. "I have more sense."

"Oh, bugga-woo!" she said.

"You promised you wouldn't!"

"Bugga-wugga-woo!"

I was having no more of that. I turned on my heel and walked off leaving her doing her ghost

50

imitation, which I didn't think was all that funny anyhow, although she did.

"I'm going to tell Kathleen that you were spying on her," I said, and I did when I got there.

Kathleen wasn't pleased!

"Have you so little to do?" she said. "You had no business following me."

"It was Breige," I said.

Her student had gone back to his digging, with the others, and we picked our way around their bits of peg and string, crossing the field from the Burnt Church graveyard to the Bloody Headland cottages.

"What are they digging for?" I asked. "Is it St. Aidan's whatsit?"

"Chalice?" she said. "No."

"Sister Consuelo said if they were working round the Burnt Church they might find it. It must be hidden somewhere."

"Melted down by some nice Cromwellian," Kathleen said.

"They didn't get it. That was why they killed all the people. They came to get it and somebody had hidden it so they killed everybody instead."

"If they killed everybody, how do you know they didn't get it?" Kathleen said.

"That's what it says in our Pageant," I said. "And Sister Consuelo says if they go on digging round the Burnt Church they might find it."

"I bet Bonaventure doesn't think so," said Kathleen.

"Sister Bonaventure?" I said.

"Sister Bonaventure is smarter than you think," said Kathleen. "She may look like an out-size frog but she has brains, which is more than you can really say for Consuelo. She was down here yesterday, Pim says, and she told Professor Meredith that he was digging in the wrong place if it was the original Christian settlements he was after. She gave him a whole speech about Irish place names, and he was livid!"

"*Pim*," I said. Your student's name is not *Pim*, surely?"

"Well, it is," she said, reddening. "I think Pim is a very nice name."

"Oh yes," I said. "Very nice!"

"You are not to tell Breige," she said, suddenly realising what I had realised already. A name like Pim is the sort of name a person like Breige could make a lot of jokes about, if she got to hear of it.

"I won't," I said.

"Cross your heart?"

"And may I burn in hell for evermore if I do," I said.

"All right," she said.

When we were on the path in front of the Bloody Headland cottages she stopped and put her glasses on. I didn't say a word, but I was glad to see them back on her nose. I'd been afraid that she would bump into something.

"I tell you what," she said. "If you promise not to tell on me. . ."

"I won't tell. I have already promised."

"All right. You promise not to tell Breige and I will take you with me this afternoon when I am going to Mrs. Annett's, and you can get your fortune told."

"Big deal," I said.

At the time I thought it wasn't, but it was.

53

Mrs. Annett lived in the new Housing Executive houses out at Tullybow, and we had to go there on our bicycles. That is, Kathleen was on her bicycle, and I was on Breige's as a result of the dishes deal. My bike is bust.

The house was a bit of a disappointment when we got there, for it was modern, not the sort of place you expect when you go to get your fortune told.

I knew why Kathleen was keen to go to a Fortune Teller all of a sudden. It was to hear all about her Pim!

"I see a stranger," Mrs. Annett said, doing her best to look mystical.

We were sitting in her front room. It was a curious room, because the furniture from her old home at the Bloody Headland cottages was all mixed up with the modern fittings of the new house. She had her old chairs and a mahogany sideboard and a piano, all made of dark wood, set against tangerine wallpaper with swirls in it, and a fluffy white carpet and a Japanese colour television set with push button hand controls, which

I suppose she paid for out of the fortune telling. The room didn't know which way it was facing, the past or the future.

She was a fussy woman, all bangles and rings, and she fussed us into the room and then said she wouldn't do our cups, no, because she didn't believe in cups, she would do us by holding our hands and looking at us. I didn't like the sound of that, because I didn't take to her, but Kathleen had already left the 50p on the hallstand that was supposed to pay for both of us, and I couldn't waste Kathleen's money. She had left the money outside because you weren't supposed to be *paying* Mrs. Annett, it was a voluntary donation, but everybody knew what the going rate was. I once heard Sister Consuelo say Mrs. Annett was a Heathen Witch Doctor, but I don't think she is as bad as that.

"You first, Kathleen," I said, and Mrs. Annett took Kathleen by the wrists and gazed into her glasses and told her about seeing a stranger.

"He will be a friend," she said. "He is well intentioned toward you."

All this was going down very well, not unex-
pectedly.

"You are to be careful," Mrs. Annett said.
"There will be other men in your life, later. The
stranger will be very dear to you, but he may not
be the One For You. I cannot see that. You will
be happy. But first you must be careful. You will
cross the big water someday, but not soon."

That seemed a safe enough bet, anyway.

"You are worried," she said. "Are you worried,
dear? This worry is not about the stranger. It is
connected to your work. Your school work?"

Kathleen nodded, but she looked put out. She
had her scent on and she was trying to make out
she was a woman of the world. Of course, Mrs.
Annett knew quite well who she was, and what
age she was for that matter. She knew Kathleen
would be in her final year, and worried about
exams.

"You will do well. You will be successful. You
may not be successful in the way you imagine.
But all will be well."

At that point I switched off. She was going

round in circles and not saying anything.

"And now the little girl," Mrs. Annett said.

I didn't like that one bit. Little, indeed! I made a face at Kathleen, as my wrists were grasped by the podgy, be-ringed hands.

"Just watch me, dear," she said. "Look into my eyes."

I looked into her eyes.

I didn't like them. They were deep eyes, a sort of greeny blue. I wondered if she put something into them to make them deep like that. Despite myself, I had an uncomfortable feeling that she was looking right through me.

"Well?" I said.

"Be still," she said firmly.

"We'll have to be getting home soon, for our tea," Kathleen said, when this had gone on for a minute or two. She wasn't so interested in speeding things up when it was dark strangers and crossing the big water!

Mrs. Annett paid no attention to her. She didn't even seem to be aware of me, except that her grip kept getting tighter on my wrists.

I sat there, feeling silly.

She let go of my hands, and bowed her head.

"What are you mixed up in, child?" she asked, without raising her eyes to look at me.

"Nothing, Mrs. Annett, honestly," I said, bewildered.

"There is something. . . there *was* something. It is a very long time ago, not now. But it is muddled up with now, somehow. I don't understand that. There is fear. There is blood." She closed up at that. I could almost feel her thinking she had gone too far. I suppose she had visions of a visit from Sister Consuelo, or an enraged parent, if she scared the willies out of me!

"You are not to worry," she said, most unconvincingly, licking her lips. "All will be well." Then she shot me a glance which said the exact opposite, as if she was sizing up how much I could take.

By this time, I was very uncomfortable.

"Whatever this is. . . or *was*. . . the bad part of it happened a long time ago, to someone else," she said. "So you mustn't let it worry you."

58

"I won't," I said.

"I suppose I'm just a silly old woman, saying things to scare you," she said.

It was the things she hadn't said that were scaring me, and the fact that she took so long making up her mind what to say. She had gone across the room to her desk, and she pulled out a pad, on which she began to draw something. It was done very quickly, and she came back and handed it to me.

"Does this mean anything to you?" she said.

"No," I said.

"It could be a design for a Celtic brooch," she said, not very hopefully. "It looks like a brooch. I see this design as meaning something in your life. You must keep what I have drawn. Keep it safely. It will have meaning for you."

"Well, thank you very much," I said, weakly, folding the paper and putting it into my anorak pocket.

"We really must get home, Mrs. Annett," Kathleen butted in, restlessly.

"That's all I can do," Mrs. Annett said, ignoring Kathleen, and talking only to me. "But you must come to me again, if you need any help. I'll do anything I can. Anything at all." She was holding my hand again in her podgy grip, and I didn't like it. She was trying to be helpful, but I wanted away from her and her funny half-then half-now house.

"If I could speak to *you* for a moment, dear, *alone*," Mrs. Annett said, turning to Kathleen, who was beginning to resent all the attention I was getting.

I went outside. It was very cold, though the snow had melted, but I didn't want to stay in Mrs. Annett's house.

I had expected to be told I was going to be rich and marry a millionaire pop-singer and cross the big water, not all this mumbo jumbo that didn't mean anything.

Kathleen came out, closing the door firmly behind her. She took a deep breath as she climbed on her bicycle, and I must say I sympathised.

"We're never coming here again," I said.

"Uhuh," she said.

We pedalled down the road.

"Well?" I asked.

She had obviously been rehearsing what she was going to say, because it came out too pat.

"She was telling me private things. Things about. . . . You Know Who!" She tossed her head and put on a big grin to mislead me.

I was meant to think it was Pim they had been talking about. That was like Kathleen. She said "You Know Who" so that she wouldn't have to tell me a lie, but it wasn't "You Know Who" they had been talking about.

It was me.

It was me, even though she wouldn't say so.

It was me, and I wanted to know what they had been saying.

Chapter Seven

We were no sooner off the bicycles when Breige came bouncing out of the house into the yard.

"Your hens are sick," she said.

"What!"

"Cocci. . . cocci. . . coccidiosis!" Breige said, cheerfully, and she added, as an afterthought; "It's infectious."

"What's cocci. . . whatever you said?" Kathleen wanted to know.

"Parasites," Breige said. "Emer's hens have wee bugs. Baldie Bannon is in the house, and he says so. He says they might all get it, and then you'll have no hens. He took a ride into Tullyvan-net on the famous bicycle and now he is back with Dettol and ammonia and he's going to help you scrub out the hen-house."

"Oh no," I said.

"Oh yes," said Breige. "And there's no need to kick my bicycle like that, just because you're cross, Emer! Dettol and ammonia! It'll make a great stink, won't it?"

"And I thought the old things were broody," I said, bitterly. It was the right time of the year for them to be broody. I had never heard of cocci-whatever-it-was.

"Baldie will tell you all about it," Breige said.

Baldie did, at his usual rate of two words every five minutes. Then we went down to the hen-house.

It was much worse than I had thought it would be.

Hen dirt is bad enough, but I am used to hen dirt. It was the scrubbing out that really got me.

Hot water, Dettol, and ammonia, all steaming round me. There I was, lying half in and half out of the hen-house, scrubbing away at the walls and floor and the roosting rack, and in between keeping an ear open for Baldie's instructions.

"That will do," he said.

"Will it?" I said, crawling out on my tummy. I was reeking with the stuff.

He poked his head into the hen-house, hat and all, and took another look round. Then he pulled his head out, and straightened himself up, one bone at a time.

"It will do," he said.

"And will the hens be all right?" I asked. He had already removed the worst infected ones, and I was glad I had missed that parting, for I like my hens.

"They might," he said.

"Do you think they'll all get it?" I asked, anxiously.

"You never know," he said.

"Well," I said. "Thanks anyway. I mean, thanks awfully Bal. . . Mr. Bannon. You have been a big help, and I am very grateful."

"Never mind that," he said, and off he went on his bicycle. He wouldn't come into the house for a cup of tea, and mumbled into his muffler when my Mother came out and offered it to him.

"He is a peculiar old customer," she said. "But

he is a good Christian neighbour to help you with your hens like that, Emer."

We went into the house. They had kept my tea in the range oven for me.

"You are not sitting down to eat like that, not in this house, Emer!" my Mother said, firmly.

"Oh, *Mammy*!" I said, for I was starving.

"Bath, Emer!" ordered my Mother. "And be sure you clean up after you. You'd better throw the old things you are wearing out, for they will be no use to man or beast."

"Bugga-wugga-woo, niffy!" Breige sang out, when I passed her on the stairs.

I got into the bath and had a good soak, then I got out and doused myself all over with Kathleen's Femme De Nuit perfume, because I couldn't believe that the smell of hot ammonia and hen dirt was really gone.

"What have you got on?" Peter said, when I came down.

"Soap," I said.

"Just soap?" said Breige, with a glint in her eye.

"All right," I said. "I took a drop out of Kathleen's blue bottle. What she doesn't know won't hurt her."

"It is a good thing for you that she is away out with her student," Breige said.

"I am fed up with you going on at me," I said, crossly.

"Oh bugga-woo!" she snorted, and off she went, upstairs. Bugga-woo was her joke for the day, along with Kathleen's glasses. Breige is like that. Sometimes it gets on my nerves.

I sat down to tea. Peter was sitting in my Father's chair by the range, and he helped himself to a cup of tea from the pot.

"I had to move your gull, Emer," Peter said. "Don't jump down my throat now! I had to!"

"Why?"

"Because Hector was going to turf it out of the hidey hole, if I hadn't!" he said.

"Hector doesn't know about the hidey hole!" I objected.

"Of course Hector knows about the hidey hole," he said scornfully. "Hector knows every

66

blade of grass round here, just as Baldie does. Wasn't he born and reared here, the same as any of us? Your hidey hole may be a secret from the strangers, but not to anyone local. He knows about the hole, and this morning he decided to move his eggs from the old houses to the hidey hole, in case Sergeant Benny Cunningham came round again."

"Oh," I said. "*What* eggs?"

"Hector's eggs. The eggs he's been smuggling, dafty! They were all over the lane when he crashed. So we moved them up to the old houses, and this afternoon he's been hiding them in the hidey hole, out of the way of Sergeant Benny Cunningham and the Customs men."

"Smuggling!" I said. "But people don't smuggle here any more. Not since the boats used Butter Point in the war."

"That's all you know," Peter said. "You get a bigger Common Market subsidy on the other side of the border, in the Republic of Ireland. Taking eggs across is big business."

"Oh," I said. So much for Hector's teasing about

my few dozen eggs. No wonder the Sergeant had been after him.

"Anyway, I'm sorry about the hidey hole, because old Baldie will be mad if he finds out, and now we owe him a favour, don't we?"

"Yes," I said. And then, "What about our poor gull? What have you done with it?"

"It's still in the hole," he said. "Only in a different bit."

"Different bit?" I said. "I didn't know there was one."

"Oh yes," Peter said. "Hector showed it to me one time. You have only to move a few stones. There are two more rooms up the back, but don't let on to Hector I told you. I had to put the old gull somewhere, and what Hector doesn't know won't hurt him."

"Secret rooms?" I said.

"Sort of. Only not so secret. I'll show you, don't worry."

"And our gull took no hurt?"

"Right as rain," he said. "Breige was up there and fed him."

The foot print in the hidey hole was explained anyway; it had been Hector prospecting for his egg-hideout.

"If Baldie finds out that Hector has taken possession of his hidey hole there will be trouble," I said. "He will do his nut."

"Baldie might do his nut, but he will not tell the Sergeant or the Customs," said Peter. "And that is all Hector is worried about. On Monday he'll have the van back on the road, and we will move the eggs on, and nobody will be any the wiser. Smuggling is a way of life down here, and why wouldn't it be, with the Republic just the other side of the Lough?"

"I don't know," I said. "I don't like it. You shouldn't have helped them."

"What harm is there in it?" Peter said.

Chapter Eight

Peter had gone upstairs to bed. I was in the scullery, getting Mammy's tray ready. I leave out a tray on the nights when I know she will be late at the hotel, so that she can have a cup of tea to warm her up after the bike ride home.

I came back into the kitchen and put the kettle on the hob. I was in the middle of doing it when I sensed that Breige had come down into the kitchen.

"No more bugga-wooing tonight," I said, snappily. "If you dare bugga-woo me once more Breige McAnna, I'll scream."

I turned round to see what she was doing, coming up on me quietly like that.

It wasn't Breige.

The Ghost was standing there, in the middle of

our kitchen, holding something cradled in her frail arms.

She was holding the doll.

Her doll.

I could see her as well as I could see the hall door, but I could see the door *through* her. I remember thinking how funny it was, and how it really wasn't funny at all.

She was cradling the doll in her tiny arms, her long hair flowing to her waist, her face pale and pathetic in its thinness.

"What. . . what do you want me to do?" I heard myself say, with the straightforward idea that there was something she wanted me to do, or she wouldn't keep appearing.

She raised her head, and looked straight at me. She had dark, frightened eyes, like a kitten. She moved forward, without seeming to move, and the doll she had been clutching she now held out toward me. She held it out to me as if she wanted me to have it. . .

. . . and then she disappeared.

Chapter Nine

I went upstairs to our room, feeling very shaken indeed. Shaken, not frightened, though I should have been frightened too, I suppose. She looked so small and defenceless that it was difficult to be frightened of her. I wanted to help her.

The doll was on the window ledge where I had left her. Breige hadn't moved her again, she had got the message after the first time.

I crossed the room and touched the doll's battered face. She was solid enough, no seeing through her. She was cold to the touch.

"Hi," Breige said. She was lying on her bed with her knees up, reading.

I replaced the doll on the window ledge, and stood there wondering what I'd got myself mixed up in.

"Hi, spooks!" Breige said cheerfully, putting down her book. It wasn't worth a reply. I went over to my bed and sat down.

"Emer," Breige said, sitting up and putting her best dramatic face on. "Speak to me, Emer!"

"Don't go on at me, Breige," I said. She must have realised from my tone of voice that something had happened. She got off her bed and came over to me.

'Emer?" she said, touching my shoulder.

"I'm all right," I said. "Honestly, I am."

"You don't look well," she said, getting very concerned all of a sudden. Considering how annoying she had been all day, it wasn't before time! "Are you sure you aren't feeling ill?"

"Yes."

"Yes, you are ill or yes you're sure?" she said, reverting to her argumentative self.

"Oh, Breige," I said, and then suddenly it all spilled out of me, not worked out properly or anything, so that it must have sounded stupid. I didn't want to tell her, not then, because I was still feeling anti-Breige, but she is my sister, and the person I talk to most about everything. It was too big a thing not to talk to somebody about, and Breige was there.

"That's it, all of it, Breige," I said. "What do you think I should do?"

She waited a minute before replying.

"You wouldn't be pulling my leg, would you?" she said, at last.

"I know what I saw, Breige. But I don't know what she wants me to do about it."

"About what?"

"I don't know about what," I said, irritably. "If I did, I wouldn't be asking you, would I?"

"Yes. . . w-e-l. . l. . . I'll tell you what," Breige said uncertainly. "You get into bed. I'll go down and make you a hot drink. Maybe I'll bump into your ghost too."

"I don't think you will," I said.

"I'm not scared of ghosts," she said, obviously trying to make light of it and buck me up, and at the same time wondering how long it would be until Mammy came in, to take the worry of having a mad sister off her hands.

She went downstairs, leaving me alone with the doll.

Nothing happened.

I couldn't sit there forever, so I got into bed, after the quickest undressing act in the history of Northern Ireland. Our room is not bad, but it is south-east facing, and takes the wind off the Lough.

Breige brought me up a cup of hot orange juice and stood over me as I drank it, like a kid taking Junior Aspirin.

"No bugga-woos in the kitchen this time," she said, but she meant it well. Then she went over toward the doll, and scooped it up from the window ledge. "I'm going to put this thing away for a while, Emer, if you don't mind," she said, trying to sound very decisive.

"No," I said, equally firmly. Hiding the doll was the last thing I wanted anyone to do. The doll was the link I had with my ghost.

"You're sure?" Breige said, doubtfully.

"You think there's something odd about it too, don't you?" I said. "Otherwise you wouldn't keep trying to get rid of it. So it isn't just me!"

"I know it is upsetting you," she said, and she put the doll down. "That's why I don't like it. Now you've started imagining ghosts. . . this is getting serious! If you go on, I'll have to get Kathleen, or Mammy or something."

"Oh no!" I said. "Don't do that! No, listen, Breige! I told you about it because, well, you're here, aren't you? And I had to tell someone. But I'm not mad! I have seen something, and you mustn't upset Mammy, or start Kathleen off, because she's bound to tell Mammy. Listen, Breige. . . I think my ghost has a *problem* and she has to tell someone and for some reason. . . I don't know why. . . I'm elected! It's the old doll, I think. . . but I can't just throw her doll away and forget her, can I?"

"Can't you?" said Breige.

"No, I can't!" I said. "You wouldn't walk out on me if I was in trouble, and I can't walk out on her."

"That's different," Breige said. She had obviously decided to be decisive and practical in the

76

face of a nutty sister.

"How different?"

"Well, for starters, you're not a ghost, are you? I can see you. You're real. Ghosts aren't. I don't believe in ghosts. I don't believe you saw one! So there!"

I couldn't get to sleep, which was hardly surprising. The doll wouldn't let me. It was the second night that had happened. I lay in the darkness trying to think about nuns and Pageants and anything but ghosts, but the doll kept watching me from the window ledge.

I turned over on my back, so that I couldn't see it, but that didn't work, because it seemed like a betrayal of the poor little thing who wanted me to help her. Help her to do what, for goodness sake?

"Try to go to sleep, Emer," Breige said, softly. It was good of her to stay awake, just for me. Maybe she was waiting until Mammy came in, to tell all and have me whisked off in the big white van.

"Breige," I said.

"Yes?"

"Promise you won't tell anyone?" I said. "Please?"

There was a long pause.

"All right," she said. "I promise. *Now* will you try to get some sleep?"

I don't know if I went to sleep, but I do know that suddenly I was very much awake and sitting up in bed and staring at the window pane above the doll's head.

"There," I said, "can't you see it?"

"No," Breige said, doubtfully.

"It's the brooch!" I said. "The brooch pattern Mrs. Annett drew for me! Look. . ." And I shoved my piece of paper down on the window ledge, beneath what was left of the image on the damp pane. The trouble was, it was disappearing. The shape was, I mean. It was as if someone had run a finger across the pane, tracing the shape. Now it was dissolving.

"There's a ring round the outside on your bit of paper," Breige pointed out. "That isn't on the glass, is it? The rest is a bit the same, but not much really."

"There's the wee dip at the beginning, and then the two lines. . . only they are much bigger, and much firmer this time."

"But it's not the same, Emer," Breige said. "It's almost as different as can be. And there's a smudge thing at the end there that isn't on your paper, and no ring round it, and the two lines are immense on this one, and just faint on Mrs. Annett's. . . so I don't think it is at all the same. And if it were it is probably just coincidence."

"What is?" I said. "You admit *something* has been written on the window then, don't you? And if something has been written on there, then somebody must have written it, mustn't they?"

"Wind," she said.

"Huh!"

"It's no go, Emer! You're not convincing me that a few marks on the window mean you have been seeing ghosts, and that's flat."

"Look at it!"

"There's nothing left to look at," she said. "Not that there ever was. It was just your imagination. You're getting me as bad as yourself!"

She was right. The image on the window had faded. But it had been there. I'd seen it.

We got back into bed, and Breige put out the light. I tucked my torch back under the pillow, where I could have it handy. We both lay in the darkness, both awake, but both pretending to be asleep.

"Emer," she said. "You awake?"

"Yes."

"Emer, you know, there can't be anything ghostly going on," she said, propping herself on one elbow and looking at me across the gap between our beds. "You don't really believe all this, do you? You are just having me on."

"I don't know what to believe," I said.

"*There are no ghosts*," she said. "That old doll has given both of us notions, that's all. It is a spooky sort of thing. It is making us think there might be ghosts."

I didn't say anything. She was talking herself into believing me.

"I don't like that old doll. It's spooky."

"If you don't believe in ghosts, then it can't be spooky," I said. "You can't have it both ways."

"I don't want it either way," she said, lying back against her pillow.

"Let's go to sleep."

"Let's."

I turned on my side, and lay there with my back to the doll and the window. I had had enough for one night.

"Emer?"

"Yes?"

"Do you mind if I put the light on again, Emer?" she said. "Just till we get to sleep?"

Chapter Ten

It was very early morning when I woke up. I switched Breige's light off, and lay there listening to her breathing.

Light. There was a bright glowing light casting the shadow of the doll across the floor of the room and up the wall, so that her head touched our Life Saving Certificates framed on the wall.

I got out of bed and padded across to the window, to see the light.

The Burnt Church was blazing red. Fingers of flame fanned out round it, almost too bright to look at. Burning. . . but it *couldn't* be! It had been burned once already, by Cromwell's men, hunting for St. Aidan's Chalice.

Burning, blazing red. . . and then the sun rose above the wall of the church, flashing straight into my eyes and blinding me for a moment, staining the sky a gorgeous shade of strawberry red.

Chapter Eleven

"I think I might be going to be a nun," Breige announced at breakfast time. It was Sunday morning, so I suppose she thought it was a topical subject, unless I had driven her to a decision with my Ghosties and Ghoulies and Things That Go Bump in the Night. "I think I might be."

She had her bright-eyed look on, and she glanced around the table waiting for us all to swoon at her feet and tell her how wonderful she was, and a credit to the Parish.

"Give us some more sugar," said Peter, busily stirring his cup.

I started to pass him the sugar bowl but Kathleen said: "You'll get it when you ask for it properly."

Peter looked hard at her, then he stretched

across the table for it himself, shifting his chair to get the extra reach. He is going to be a big man like my Father when he grows up, so my Mother says.

"You have the manners of an elephant in Fossett's Circus," Kathleen said.

"I said I'm going to be a nun," Breige said, making sure to raise her voice so that we would all hear her.

"What sort of a nun?" asked Kathleen, looking at the clock. We were due at Mass at half past. We have to catch the bus at the Bloody Headland which takes us into Tullyvannet.

"I am writing away to the Holy Sisters of Saint Alvarez La Garcia," said Breige. "They're in Brazil," she added, as a casual afterthought.

"*Brazil*!" exclaimed Kathleen, rising beautifully to the bait.

"Brazil," said Breige, deeply satisfied that she had made an impression at last.

"Breige McAnna you will do no such thing as write to any nuns in Brazil!" Kathleen said, indignantly. "Do you want Mammy to have a fit?"

"I've already done it," said Breige, all shining eyed.

"*Breige*!" exclaimed Kathleen, in horror.

"That'll please Sister Consuelo and no mistake," I said, wrily.

"You're too young," Peter pointed out.

"I'm not," said Breige. "I got it out of the St. Patrick's Missions Magazine. I am not too young. I am just right to be thinking about my Vocation." And with that she helped herself to another cup of tea and a piece of soda bread.

"It is all coffee in Brazil," I said. "And you don't like coffee."

"Huh!" said Kathleen, fiercely.

It was nearly a quarter past when we left the house, so we were a bit late. We would have been later still if my Mother hadn't got up out of bed and chased us out. She had to get her sleep, so she went to Evening Mass.

We got to the Bloody Headland before the bus, with Breige and Kathleen arguing all the way, as good a start as any to a peaceful Sunday.

"Well," Breige said. "What are we going to do

about it?"

We were on our way home, and Mikey Samuel had given us a lift as far as the top of Hogan's Lane. Given Breige and me a lift, that is, for Peter had to go on into Tullyvannet for his hurling and Kathleen had fish of her own to fry, not unconnected with her friend Pim.

"About what?" I said, trudging down the lane.

"Your ghost," she said.

"I thought you didn't believe in ghosts," I said.

"I don't," Breige said. "At least I don't *think* I do. But I know you do, and you're all upset about it, and I suppose that means I have to help you sort things out, whether I believe in ghosts or not. Honestly, you should have seen your face last night when you came up from the kitchen! I thought you were going to drop dead on the spot. I was getting ready to resuscitate you, the way we learned down at the pool last summer. And then there were the marks on the pane. I don't know. . . there were some marks, it wasn't just the wind. And I don't believe you made the marks just to scare me, and they *were* a bit like the ones on the bit of paper Mrs. Annett gave you. . . well, if that is true, then it could all be true, couldn't it? So where do we start?"

"I don't know," I said.

"Oh," she said.

"I suppose, if we have to start looking, we should begin where all this trouble began, don't you?"

"I'm game if you are," Breige said.

Easier said than done. You can't just rush out to somebody's ditch and start digging holes in it, especially when you don't own the ditch, and it is near enough to the road for your neighbours to see you and ask what you are digging for.

"What are we digging for?" Breige asked. "I mean supposing somebody asks us?"

"My brooch," I said.

"What brooch? The one Mrs. Annett drew? The one in your drawing?"

I shook my head. "The brooch I dropped when we were standing round Hector's van," I said. "I wouldn't like to lose it."

"Did you drop a brooch?"

"Of course I didn't," I said. "But it will do to cover us, won't it?"

We were up at the hidey hole, where Breige had shown me the hidden bit.

It wasn't all that difficult to get into. The passage narrowed down very much, so that you had to wriggle your way between two big stones, and come in sideways. Somebody unknown had put a number of small stones over the gap, and I had never known it was there. I felt a bit mortified, and at the same time I was annoyed that Baldie had never shown it to me.

"I expect Baldie thinks this bit isn't safe," Breige said, when we had both squeezed through.

It was certainly dark and dismal enough, a low-roofed passage running away into the dark.

"On here," Breige said, and we moved forward in the light of my torch, till we came to a blank end, where there was a wall of loose stone. There were two small rooms one on each side of the passage. Peter had moved our gull into one of them.

The gull didn't seem to mind it. He was on the sack cloth which Breige and Peter had arranged for him, and the torch didn't put him off at all.

"Gull!" I said. "Gull!"

"Gull is a stupid name for a gull," Breige said.

"What else?" I said

"I don't know," she said. Then she shivered. "Cold down here, isn't it?"

"Yes."

"I wish this was all over. This business of yours. D'you know, Emer, I'm scared."

We waited until the people going into Tullyvannet for the Evening Mass had gone down the road, by which time it was still light, but at least there weren't so many people about. The story of the hunt for the brooch was a feeble one, and we didn't want to use it unless we had to.

"You first," Breige said.

We had decided to move the stones and dig around, like Pim and his friends, just in case. . . well, *in case*. It seemed better to do *something*, even if it was silly.

I took the spade and faced up to the broken ditch, where the shop van had banged it over.

"This is hopeless," I said, after five grotty minutes mainly taken up with heaving boulders out of the way. "I am cold, and I have had enough, and it was a rotten silly idea in the first place, this was!"

"I'll try a bit," said Breige, who had been perched on the wall, keeping watch in case anyone came along the lane.

It was beneath the second stone that she moved.

"Oh Sacred Heart! Emer!" Breige exclaimed, putting her hands to her face. "Would you look at that?"

I knelt down and touched it. It was frail, clogged with earth, terribly mottled and discoloured, with half of one side missing, but I knew what I was looking at without being told.

I was looking at a human skull.

Chapter Twelve

We kept on knocking at the cottage door, but nobody came for ages. Then, when somebody did come, it wasn't the somebody we'd been expecting.

"The Wee McAnnas?" Mrs. Bannon said, peering round the door at us. She looked so old that it was a wonder she could stand up. Baldie was nearer eighty than seventy, and she was his Mother, so she must have been very old.

"Oh", I said. "Oh. We were. . . we were looking for Baldie. . . Mr. Bannon, I mean, Mrs. Bannon."

"Come in. Come in. Alexander's out, but he'll not be a minute."

"Well, I don't know," I said, doubtfully. Perhaps coming to Baldie for help wasn't such a good idea anyhow, but we couldn't think of anybody else. I wasn't going to start telling Hector ghost stories, and my Mother was already off in Tullyvannet for the Evening Mass, and Mikey Samuel would be as bad as Hector, only worse. I didn't sort with the Smyths, and that left only Baldie. At least I could trust him to do something, though *what* was the question. Now, when we'd been expecting Baldie, all we'd got was the very ancient Mrs. Bannon.

"Come in, come on in," she said, and before we knew it, we were in.

"You are the neighbours' girls, you are," she said, with a little chuckle. "Plenty of sap in ye! You shouldn't be calling on an ould bachelor!"

I looked hopelessly at Breige. Surely she knew that Alexander was an old man, and not likely to be courting anybody, let alone us? Breige shrugged. Baldie was her only surviving son, even if he was in his seventies. Perhaps she still thought of him as a young man.

"Dickie's dead," she said. "You know my boy Dickie's dead, don't you?"

"Yes, Mrs. Bannon," I said. "We are very sorry for your trouble."

Breige made a face. Dickie had been dead since the end of the war, long before we were born.

Mrs. Bannon hobbled over to her chair by the fire. She sat down upon it with a little sigh.

"You're awful young to be out," she said.

"Yes, Mrs. Bannon," said Breige, uncomfortably.

"You'll get old, you will," she said, and she gave another cackle.

Then I heard the footsteps out the back, and Baldie came stooping into the room, ducking his head to avoid the low beam. It must have been awkward to be such a big man in such a small cottage. Now I realised why she wouldn't let us go. At the Bloody Headland Cottages their lavatories are chemical ones down the yard.

"Alex! Alex! It is the Graiguenamanagh girls come courting you!" Mrs. Bannon said, clapping her hands as though we were a Pierrot show. "Aren't you the ould goat!"

"*What* girls?" said Breige.

I looked at Baldie Bannon, afraid that he would be annoyed at us for upsetting his mother. He didn't look a bit put out.

"I have a puncture," I said, telling a quick lie to get him away from his Mother. "I was wondering, maybe, could you fix it for me?"

"I could," he said, though he looked a bit surprised. He was too polite an old stick to say so, but he knew that I could fix any puncture that ever was, and my fingers were defter than his would ever be again. Still, he didn't bat an eyelid.

"You stay with Mrs. Bannon," I whispered to Breige. "I'll talk to Baldie. You can follow us up the road to Hogan's Lane in a minute."

"God be with you, and grant you rest," he said, touching his hat, but not removing it. Then he straightened up from the ditch.

"It isn't a sheep's skull, is it?" I said.

"It is not."

"It's. . . it's a person?" Breige asked.

"A wee child," he said.

"Oh," she said. "*Oh*," and she gave me a very

scared look. It was the first *positive* proof of what I'd been saying, and it was pretty scary.

We had been hoping. . . half hoping. . . that it was a sheep's skull, and we'd made a mistake. Now there was no mistake about it.

"What do we do now?" I said, trying to sound sensible although I was filled with all sorts of notions. . . the chief of which was a silly satisfied feeling that Breige *had* to believe me, now that we'd found my girl. It never occurred to me that it could have been someone else. I knew it wasn't.

"We should get the police, I suppose," Breige said.

"How could we explain, Breige?" I said.

I didn't want the whole Parish going on about me and my ghosts.

"If you find a body you have to get the police," Breige said.

"The child has been dead for a long time," Baldie said. His tone didn't surprise me. Baldie had no love of the police. He connected them with the government, and Winston Churchill, who had taken his land from him. None of the men round our way have much time for the police, what with smuggling and everything. It isn't a good way to be, but it is the way we are.

"Let well enough alone," he said.

"We *have* to get the police," Breige said. "Somebody's dead, after all. She might have been murdered."

If Baldie noticed the "she" he didn't say anything about it. I think he didn't notice it.

"Nobody could prove anything now," I said. "I mean, she was probably murdered by the Vikings, or someone. I expect whoever murdered her is long dead as well. Anyway, who says she was murdered? Maybe she just died."

"You don't believe that!" Breige said, turning on me.

She was right.

I was thinking of the church, burning, as the sun rose, and the shadow that the doll cast across the floor of our room. They burned the church and killed all the people. . .

"What do you think we should do, Mr.

Bannon?" I asked.

"Back in the ground," he said.

"We can't just leave her here," Breige protested. "It isn't right."

"The Holy Ground," he said.

"I ought to say something," Breige said, in her capacity as someone who was maybe going to be a nun someday.

We had come to the old grave yard at the Burnt Church, down by the sea wall, where no-one would see us. Baldie had buried the skull and the few other bone fragments we had collected.

We had taken the route along the shore to avoid the cottages, bringing what we had found with us. It felt unreal. We couldn't be doing it. The things that had happened couldn't be happening.

"Hail Mary, full of Grace," Breige started off, in a nun-like mumble. "The Lord is with thee. Blessed art thou among women and blessed is the fruit of thy womb, Jesus. Holy Mary, Mother of God, pray for us sinners, now and at the hour of our death."

"Amen," we all said.

"Your turn," she said.

"I don't know," I said. "I don't think I want to say anything."

"Prayer for the dead," Breige prompted, relentlessly.

"Eternal rest grant unto her O Lord and let perpetual light shine upon her. May her soul and the souls of all the faithful departed through the mercy of God rest in peace. Amen."

We climbed over the wall, and started back across the fields, and suddenly it wasn't so bad.

The wind died. The night sky was bright with stars, and the dark shapes of the mountains towered over the glittering water of the Lough.

"Mourne," I said. "The Mountains of Mourne. It is a funny name. You wouldn't believe it if it wasn't true."

Nobody said anything. Nobody needed to.

Chapter Thirteen

I carried the hot water bottles up to our room, and put them in our beds. Normally we don't use bottles after March, but I felt like a bit of comfort.

There was the doll. . . looking at me.

I sat down on the bed. The trouble was . . . it wasn't over. I couldn't explain why, but I knew that whatever was happening to me hadn't finished yet. There was more to come. That was why I had come up to our room on my own, leaving Breige explaining to Kathleen and Mammy that we had just been for a long walk by the Bloody Headland and there was nothing to get worked up about.

"Are you there?" I said, out loud. "If you are there, give me some sign."

Nothing happened.

"I will help you if I can, only I don't know if I can. I would help, if I knew what you wanted. It was Cromwell's people, wasn't it? The Bloody Headland time, when they burned the church?"

"Emer?" Breige said, from the doorway.

"Hi," I said. The Direct Talking Method hadn't worked. I would have been very surprised if it had. But I couldn't think of anything else to do, except wait.

"What are we going to do, Emer?" she said.

"Nothing," I said. "Unless something happens."

The ghost was in our room.

I lay in bed, too scared to move.

Breige was comfortably asleep in the other bed, her head under the blankets, a compromise she had decided to adopt instead of keeping the light on. She was too proud to do that again, because it would have looked as if she was afraid of the dark. She was, which was hardly surprising after what we'd been through, but she didn't want to know that I knew. . . .

Now the ghost was standing close to the window, by the doll.

"Is . . . is that you?" I said, out loud.

She faded away, slowly, without turning to face me.

I got up out of bed and fumbled for the torch.

The design . . . the same brooch design as before, was traced on the cold window pane.

Chapter Fourteen

"*Emer*!" said Sister Consuelo, menacingly.

"Yes, Sister," I said, coming sleepily back to Monday morning in school. It was difficult to keep awake, let alone keep my mind on what she was saying.

"What was I talking about, Emer?" Sister Consuelo said. "Perhaps you could recapitulate for the benefit of anyone in the class who may not have been listening."

"It was about the Bishop," I said.

"Emer says it was about the Bishop," Sister Consuelo said, nipping her thin lips together. "Now she is going to tell us *what* about the Bishop, aren't you Emer?"

"About the Bishop coming," I said, not very hopefully. "Tomorrow. What we are to do when the Bishop comes."

"And what are we to do, Emer?"

I looked around desperately. There was no help from anyone.

"Dress up," I said. "Like Vikings and monks. And. . . and Cromwell burning the Church, and hiding St. Aidan's Chalice and everything, so they couldn't find it."

"Oh Emer, dear," she said, wearily. Then she turned away from me with a hopeless shrug. "I'll have to consider what to do about you, Emer," she said. "I'll have to think it over very seriously. You simply are not attending. *Now*, for your benefit, and the benefit of other dreamers, I will repeat what I have already said."

And she did.

I knew from the look of her that I was for it, this time! She would give me a note for my Mother saying I wasn't paying attention at school, and that would be awful. And it wasn't my fault at all. How could I be interested in the old Pageant and St. Aidan's Chalice and whatever when I was in the middle of something much worse?

"And tomorrow, mind, nobody is to be late," Sister Consuelo finished up. "You are to be early, and your costumes are to be clean, and mind your ps and qs, girls."

No word about a note, yet. She would need time to write one that would really pin my ears back!

"What are ps and qs?" Breige asked, as we were going down the corridor to the Dinner Room.

"Don't know," I said, unhappily.

"Walk, girls," Sister Consuelo's voice echoed down the corridor after us.

"She would have made a good Viking," I said.

Half past two, and no note!

I looked across at Breige, and she gave me a double fingers crossed sign. Maybe I was going to get away with it.

"Emer!" Sister Bonaventure blinked at me over her glasses.

"Sister?"

"Perhaps you can assist the class with this one.

Emer," she said, writing on the board.

GRAIGUENAMANAGH

Was I supposed to know it? We were onto townland names, which is a subject Sister Bonaventure likes. She is a nun you can get to talk, and then you don't have to do any work for ages and ages. Actually, she is interesting sometimes, but not always. I had a feeling this was one of the "not always's".

"Well, Emer?"

"Please Sister, please, I know." Sally Doran piped up from the back. She would. She does Irish speaking at the Feis. A Feis is a competition we have, where people do Irish things like dancing and playing traditional instruments and verse speaking. Sally is always going on about Irish because she is a show-off.

"I said Emer," said Sister Bonaventure, her round eyes blinking behind her glasses.

"I don't know it, Sister," I said.

"I do," said Sally.

"Let's see, where's your better half. . . Breige

106

McAnna, can you help your sister out on this one?"

"No, Sister," said Breige.

"I know! I know why it's them!" Sally said.

"Dear, dear, girls, you've let me down," Sister said. "Perhaps Sally can give us a clue, can you Sally? Tell us why the McAnna girls should know this one."

"Because they live there!" said Sally, all pleased with herself.

"Right, again, Sally," said Sister, sounding not-very-pleased. The thing is that Sally is always the star pupil when it comes to Irish bits. "Now then, GRAIGUENAMANAGH. What do you suppose it means?"

"Please Sister, no Sister," I said.

"What?"

"Please Sister, no Sister." I said, glad to get putting Sally in her place. "We don't live at that place, that Sally said. We live at Craggy Man. You know we live at Craggy Man, Sister."

"*Graig*uena*man*agh" Sister Bonaventure said, putting stress on the word.

"Oh," I said, catching on. The thing is that when the English came to Ireland, they often couldn't pronounce Irish – neither can I! – and so they said the nearest thing to it. So Sally was probably right after all. "Graiguenamanagh" would be "Craggy Man".

"And it means. . .?" said Sister Bonaventure, looking round the class. "Who can tell me what it means?"

"The Village of the Monks," said Sally.

"Correct," said Sister Bonaventure. "Which brings me to the subject of the Bishop's Pageant. In all probability, to judge by the townland name, if there is a settlement to be found near the mouth of the Lough, it will be in that immediate area."

"Oh," I said, sitting up.

"Were you trying to say something, Emer?" Sister Bonaventure asked.

"No, Sister," I said, remembering that I had to be on my best behaviour.

"It would follow that the true site of the events depicted in your Pageant was in and around the McAnnas' home."

108

"Please Sister, what about the excavating?" Mary Toner said, from the back of the class.

Sister Bonaventure gave a wide grin. When she grinned her glasses moved on her nose, making her look more like a frog than ever. "If I had been consulted, and I was not, I would have told them that all they are likely to dig up down on the Bloody Headland are the cottage drains and anything that Mr. Cromwell's men left behind them!"

"Please Sister, there are no drains," Breige said.

"In that case," Sister Bonaventure said, "all they'll get will be the butchered bones of the poor souls who died there, giving the place its name, Bloody Headland."

"What about the Chalice, Sister?" Mary said.

I wasn't paying attention to her. Skiddy Rice was at the door, trying to get in, and she was holding one of Sister Consuelo's envelopes in her hand.

My heart went down into my boots!

"It is my pious hope that the Chalice will be

recovered, some day," said Sister, going to the door. "But it is my belief that it was taken and melted down at the time of the sacking of the church. The legend that it was taken from the church and hidden in the surrounding neighbourhood is typical of its time, but unlikely to have any basis in truth. Yes, Teresa?"

She had swung open the door. Skiddy – her real name is Teresa but we call her Skiddy – Skiddy handed in the note.

"Emer?" Sister said.

"Yes, Sister."

"I have a note here addressed to your Mother. Would you be good enough to deliver it?"

Chapter Fifteen

"You could emigrate to Australia on my bicycle," Breige said.

We were coming back home across the airfield. The note was burning a hole in the pocket of my anorak.

"Suicide," I said, trying to be cheerful about it, when I didn't feel cheerful at all.

"That's a mortal sin," Breige pointed out.

"Have they got any spare cloisters in that Convent you wrote to in Brazil?" I asked. "Room for a little inattentive Irish nun?"

"Plus ghost," Breige said.

"Plus ghost."

"I didn't really write," she said. "I just said I had to see what Kathleen would say."

I didn't believe Breige for a minute. She had

written to Brazil all right. When she saw we all thought she was mad she was trying to back-track on it and make it look as if she was playing one of her jokes on Kathleen.

I didn't really care. I wasn't in a jokey mood.

I was terribly upset about the note. Not because I'd done something awful. I hadn't raided the poor-box or stolen the crown jewels or thrown my dinner at Sister Consuelo; all I'd been doing was not listening much, when I should have been doing the star pupil bit. It wasn't fair to give me a note home for a little thing like that.

The trouble wasn't me, so much; it was Mammy. She had enough to put up with, without a note home as well. She would think I was carrying on because I was upset about having no Father and her going out to work and she would start telling me about how we needed the money otherwise she wouldn't be doing it and she would go on about not being a proper mother again. She *is* a proper mother. She's a lovely mother, but she does get upset about us sometimes, and I couldn't argue with the note, could I? If Consuelo said I wasn't working, I wasn't working. Anyway, I wasn't.

Mammy was in the house.

"I have this note for you, Mammy," I said, and handed it straight over.

Breige made a fast exit up the stairs to our room.

"Note?" Mammy said, and she took it from me.

She was sitting at the table. I stood at the far end of it from her, stock still, knowing what Mary Queen of Scots must have felt like before they cut her head off.

Mammy slit open the envelope with the kitchen knife.

I closed my eyes.

"Well, isn't that nice! That beats all!" she said.

I opened my eyes.

"We've won a bottle of whiskey in the St. Martin's White Missionaries Baptismal Fund Raffle!" she said.

It must have been the relief that did it!

I came down the back stairs and out into the

yard to check the hens and suddenly something clicked. I went straight up the stairs again and got the piece of paper Mrs. Annett had given me.

I spread it out on the window ledge, beside the stumpy figure of the doll, then I got another piece of paper and drew the shapes that had appeared on the window. They were almost, but not quite, the same. There was a ring round the whole thing in Mrs. Annett's sketch, and the two lines that cut the sketch in half were much firmer and bolder in the ghost's efforts, even though they had been weakly traced on damp glass.

I sat there a long time, thinking about it.

A lot of things were jumbled up. Sister Bonaventure and Cromwell and the drains and Graigeunamanagh being "Village of the Monks" and Baldie Bannon's hidey hole and our gull and Mrs. Annett's "*Fear*" and "*Blood*" and what I'd seen through the window when the sun came up behind the Church and I thought it was burning all over again. That was an accident, of course. . . I just happened to be looking out of the window at the right minute. . . one of many accidents and

114

coincidences. Too many.

Like the condensation making the doll "cry". . . like the gull being in the hidey hole. . . like Hector hiding his eggs there, and Peter moving the gull to the other chamber. . . like finding the skull. . . like the church burning in the sun. . . like Sister Bonaventure and her *"Butchered bones."*

No accidents, no coincidences. Ever since I'd picked up her doll she had been using me. There was something she wanted me to do . . . and now I thought I knew what it was.

Chapter Sixteen

"Right," said Breige. "Fire away! I'm listening."

We were standing on the slight slope behind Bannon's houses, facing up toward the hidey hole. Standing where I'd first seen the ghost, when she was advancing toward it.

"It isn't a hidey hole," I said. "It is a souterrain. One of the places that the monks used, for hiding things."

"A souterrain?" Breige said, sounding unconvinced.

"Yes," I said. "Souterrains are supposed to have been for hiding things, and people as well sometimes. They were long underground passages with chambers opening off them, and they were usually difficult to get into, so that if you were inside and an invader was outside you could have a free bash at him as he squeezed in. Well, the entrance to the inner bit of the hidey hole fits that description! And this is the Village of the Monks, Sister says so. We know they had souterrains, and this is one of them."

"*You* think," Breige said. "*I* think it is Baldie Bannon's hidey hole."

"It is," I said, triumphantly.

"You said it was a souterrain!"

"That's right. It's *both*, don't you see? It is Baldie Bannon's hidey hole now, and it was a souterrain then, that's all. It's the same hole, and people are still hiding things in it! It is full of eggs this minute, and the invaders, that's Benny Cunningham and the Customs men, can't find it. So it is still doing what a souterrain did, and it is still Baldie's hidey hole."

"I hope he doesn't find out about the eggs," Breige said, still not taking me seriously.

"Don't bother about that now," I said. "This is much more important."

"What is?"

"My ghost is," I said. "Don't you see, it is the

117

hidey hole I've been getting all my messages about."

"What messages?" she said, bewildered.

"The drawings – the thing on the window pane – that Mrs. Annett thought was a brooch. She was so sure that what she was seeing was a brooch that she ended up drawing a brooch shape round it. . . but she was wrong. It isn't a brooch!"

"Okay," Breige said. "What is it, then?"

"It's a map," I said.

"*What*?"

"A map."

"What of?"

"Of the souterrain. *This* souterrain."

"Oh," Breige said.

"It doesn't look like this souterrain, I'll admit," I said.

"It certainly doesn't. This souterrain has one little room and then the narrow stones and then two little rooms, but there's more in your map, isn't there? There's a whole other bit, beyond those lines. . . oh!"

"You know what is in here, don't you?" I said,

as we squeezed through the rocks into the narrow passageway. "At the end of the passage? Remember the first day we came? The walls are firm, except for the end. The walls are loose stone there. They're loose stone because they aren't walls!"

"Come again?"

"The two lines on the drawing, marked very firmly across the souterrain, represent the place where the passage is blocked. But it isn't blocked by a wall. Look at it!"

Breige put out her hand, and felt the stones. They certainly blocked the passage, but they were not shaped and worked into position as the walls that ran up to them were.

"The people who built souterrains were good stoneworkers," I said. "They would never have put up a pile of old rubble like that."

"Who did then?"

"No-one did!"

"Somebody did. I mean, here it is!"

"No," I said. "Roof fall!"

"Oh," she said.

"And beyond the roof fall, there is a further chamber. And in the other chamber. . ."

"Is what?"

"You remember Sister Consuelo, and the legend? The legend Sister Bonaventure says is a load of old rubbish? How the Chalice was taken from the Church before Cromwell's marauders came, and hidden near the Bloody Headland? And it is supposed to have been a child that did it, isn't it? Well, Breige, I *believe* the legend."

"But it isn't true," she objected. "Sister Bonaventure said. . ."

"Sister Bonaventure said it was unlikely, not impossible. Well, I say it is *likely*, and I'm going to find out."

"How?"

"You and I are going to move these stones, and get through to the other chamber."

"*If* there is one. *If* this is a souterrain. *If* there has been a roof fall. *If* you ever saw a ghost at all."

"Yes."

"A typical Emer exercise!" she snorted.

But she set to and helped me. We moved the stones quickly, tossing them back behind us into the tunnel.

It wasn't just stone. There was dust and rubble as well. Goodness knows how long ago the roof had collapsed. The other problem was that as we took stones out, others simply fell into position.

"Help!" Breige said. "The things you get me into, Emer."

"Come on," I said.

Her face was streaked with sweat and dirt, where she had wiped her brow. I was pretty ruined myself, but I kept going.

If the Chalice was there. . .

"Emer," Breige said, stopping work again. "Emer, I think that we're weakening this thing with every stone we pull out. It collapsed in the first place, I know, but it has had years and years and years to settle. Now we are disturbing it. It might fall."

"Do you want to give up?" I said.

"Well. . ." she said, doubtfully.

"You just don't want to believe me," I said.

"You're *chicken*!"

"No I'm not," she said, and we went back to work, tugging and pulling and scraping at the fallen stones, gradually clearing a way through. It was hard work, because they had settled firmly over the years, but there was now no question in my mind that it was a roof fall, and not something built by the same people who had built the souterrain.

Which meant that there was a second chamber and, if I was right, in that second chamber was St. Aidan's Chalice.

"You wait, Breige," I muttered between gritted teeth. . . there was grit in my mouth as well. . . "You wait. If the Chalice is there we'll be absolutely the most famous people ever."

Then my hand went through.

Right through. . .

. . . through to the other side!

"Breige!" I breathed, and she joined me, helping to drag the stones and dirt clear.

Then I got my arm in, and part of my head. . . and the air was fresh, so there had to be another

122

opening. I got my head fully through, but I couldn't see much. Then my shoulders, and with a wriggle I was through. Breige's head came through, and she reached out for me. I took her arm and heaved her forward.

Something moved above us.

"*Breige*!" I cried out. "Breige, quick!"

And then it all came down. The whole thing seemed to collapse around us, smothering us and burying us in choking dust and heavy earth and stone.

Chapter Seventeen

I was in pain.

There was something lying on my neck, and I could hardly breathe. I had one hand free, and I brought it to my throat. There was a sharp stone against my throat, and when I tried to move it cut into me.

My mouth was full of dirt. I was choking, and I couldn't spit it out, for my head was forced back, and my body was twisted sideways. I had no leverage.

I was going to die.

"I'm not going to die in here!" I decided, and then I started to kick and thresh and kick and thresh and then something gave way and my hand was round the stone, and something was pressing hard against my nose, and there was a lot of dirt

in my eyes but still I was forcing myself sideways and away from the rock at my throat and then my feet pressed something and I shoved forward, and suddenly I could move my body round.

I stopped threshing. There was no pain, almost, but there was some blood, and I spat that out, and with it came a gardenful of mud. Something had sliced a bit off my tongue and I still couldn't move properly. Then I reached out behind me and managed to grab something and pull myself toward it, at the same time striking out with my legs, though the weight which had been on my chest was now on my knees.

Then I was out.

I was in the darkness, and the first thought was that something had happened to my eyes, I put my hand up and my eyes were still there and I could see my fingers when I cleared the grit so that was all right.

Breige.

Where was Breige?

"Breige! Breige! BREIGE!" I shouted. . . it must have been more a scream, for I was convinced she was in there, under what I'd just got free from, trapped, and she would be dead, and there would be no Breige anymore and it would be all my fault for bringing her in there in the first place just for a bit of excitement, when we could have got the proper archaeologists to excavate it and now she was dead and I had to get to her in case she wasn't dead but she must be dead because dead was all she could be under all that stone. . . .

. . . then I felt her.

I didn't know what bit of her it was, but it was flesh and it wasn't me so it had to be Breige and I went straight in after her feeling and groping and thrusting at the loose stone and rubble till I had her head.

"Breige," I said. "Breige!" And this time it really was a scream, because I had her head and I could feel her neck pulse and Breige wasn't breathing.

Breige wasn't breathing.

I went cold. Suddenly I could hear Mrs. Thomason's voice, repeating what she had said last summer at the cold pool.

I could hear Mrs. Thomason's voice, as if she was really there. Breige was always my partner. I resuscitated her, then she resuscitated me. Turn and turn about. And there was Mrs. Thomason's voice, against the shouting of the children in the pool.

"You must never ever resuscitate anyone unless you have to. If you do it with someone who doesn't need it the force of the air from your lungs may kill. It is a terribly terribly dangerous thing to do. Never never resuscitate unless you have no alternative, and there is no more experienced person present to do it in your place. But when you are sure that the subject has stopped breathing, you must resuscitate at once. There is no time for delay. The slightest delay may lead to brain damage or death."

Now it was Breige, and this time it wasn't to pass my Intermediate Life Saving Certificate, it was to make Breige breath again, because if I couldn't do that I had killed her.

"Calm, cool and quick."

It was all right for Mrs. Thomason, she didn't

have to do it. And the funny thing I remembered in the middle of it was that she had a bathing wrap like a monk. Monks couldn't keep out of it, even at the end.

"Breathing has stopped when the victim is unconscious and doesn't appear to be breathing."

I knew she wasn't breathing, but Mrs. Thomason wouldn't get on with it.

"You must not panic."

Not panic.

"Lie the subject on the back with the head a little higher than the feet."

I hadn't got her feet, they were somewhere in there under the rubble. I had pulled her head and body clear, as far as the hips, that would have to do.

"Tilt the head back to extend the air passage and lift the jaw forward."

Done.

Mrs. Thomason would have been pleased with me, if she could have seen me. All I had done was to kill my sister, after all.

Not kill. Breige wasn't gone yet.

"*Make sure the mouth is clear of all obstructions.*"

Great lumps of dirt came out of her mouth, and I had to thrust my fingers down her throat and stones and dirt came up from there, but I was sure I had it all. And she didn't start breathing. If I had the air passage clear, she was supposed to start breathing, that was what Mrs. Thomason said. But Breige didn't start breathing.

"*If breathing does not recommence resuscitation must start immediately.*"

It didn't recommence. She wasn't breathing. I had to have a go. You don't panic. You have to do it, and keep doing it, because if you don't they are dead. Only when I'd done it, it had been pretend, with Mrs. Thomason telling me jokes in between and Breige saying things that drowned people aren't supposed to say. It wasn't pretend this time.

Breige wasn't breathing.

But Breige wasn't dead. Not yet. She wasn't dead yet.

So I tilted her head back with one hand on the

top of her head, just as Mrs. Thomason had showed me. Then I pinched her nose closed with the fingers of that hand, still keeping her head back, took a deep breath, and bent down and closed my mouth over hers to make an air-seal.

"Five quick puffs, the first time, Emer," Mrs. Thomason said. *"Keep your fingers on her chin. Don't press on her throat."*

So I gave her the five quick puffs you have to begin with, and she didn't start breathing.

"Lean back, breathe in, and watch for movement of the chest, counting up to five as you do so. Count and breathe at the same time, and keep watching the chest."

It didn't work. She wasn't going to start breathing, ever again.

"One puff, this time, breathing deeply," Mrs. Thomason said, firmly.

I did it again, and again, counting One-Two-Three-Four-Five with Mrs. Thomason beating time beside me, watching Breige's chest each time, just the way we had done it at the pool.

Again.

Again.

Again.

And her chest began to move.

My sister Breige was breathing, and Mrs. Thomason had gone away and I was in the darkness, trying to move the top of her body sideways into the coma position so that she wouldn't choke and there was something else in the darkness, glittering, and I knew it was the Chalice we'd come looking for and at that moment I just didn't care. I had Breige's head on one side with her airways clear and she was breathing and maybe someone would find us and maybe they wouldn't but I couldn't do anything about it and Breige was breathing and that was all I could do. Maybe Peter and Hector would find us when they came to move the eggs, and maybe they wouldn't. . .

"Hullo. Hullo. . . is anyone in there?"

There was a torch beam, and Hector Hogan's voice, and he was poking his head through the hole where we'd been trapped.

And then Peter was there, and they were

moving the stones to get us out and the last thing I remember is saying; "Peter! Our gull, would you see about our gull?"

And then I passed out.

Chapter Eighteen

The next bit is hazy, which isn't surprising, I suppose, when you consider that several tons of earth and stone had dropped on my head.

I was talking to the Bishop who was standing beside my bed. I knew it was the Bishop, because I'd seen his photograph in the *Mourne Observer*. The nuns were always showing us.

Sister Consuelo and Sister Bonaventure were there as well, and my Mother, and Kathleen, all round the bed.

"Where's Breige?" I said, suddenly thinking I had killed her after all.

"Breige is all right," somebody said, and I didn't know whether to believe them or not. "She is, you know," my Mother said, and I believed her.

There was something glistening and shining at the end of the bed and the Bishop was talking to me and telling me about it.

It was the Chalice. St. Aidan's Chalice, and they were awfully pleased with me, even Sister Consuelo.

So that was all right. I'd found the Chalice. I'd been right about the ghost. She had hidden it, and then she had been killed with all the others after the Church on the Bloody Headland was burned by Cromwell's men. The Chalice had lain hidden in the souterrain for years and years until I found the wooden doll, and she came haunting me.

That's what happened to me, and how I was haunted.

I don't want to be haunted ever again.

I was all right, and Breige was all right, and we were the star pupils in the convent school for finding the Chalice so they could show off to the Bishop, and you would have thought butter wouldn't melt in our mouths, but that didn't take long to wear off. I didn't feel right till Sister

Consuelo started hounding me again!

There was one last thing.

It was the day we said goodbye to our gull. We took him down to the shore by the Burnt Church, and loosed him. He waddled away from us and took off with the wing as good as new, and never a look back.

"There's gratitude!" Breige said, but she was as glad to see him right again as I was.

Then neither of us said anything, but we went up through the broken wall and into the grave yard. It was one of those warm clear evenings, and the Lough was absolutely placid, solid blue, and there was a rightness about everything, including the little grave we'd made, down by the wall.

"I was going to bring her the doll," I said. "But then I didn't."

"She'd want you to have it, Emer," Breige said.

Then we walked home by the shore and turned in across the airfield to our house, and our mountains, talking about all the things that had happened to us.

135

"She must have been awfully brave," Breige said. "Imagine taking the Chalice from the Church and hiding it like that, with everyone being killed all around her. I'm glad you did what she wanted, and I'm sorry I laughed at you."

"Shut up, or someone will hear you!" I said. We had agreed to keep the ghost side of things to ourselves, because nobody would believe it. We went into the kitchen.

I flopped down in my Father's chair, tired out, and Breige went off to hunt for her book, upstairs.

I sat for a moment or two, head back, eyes closed, resting, feeling very at home and content, because it had been a good day and our gull was all right and there was nothing left to worry about that wouldn't come right.

Then something made me open my eyes. I had been half expecting her anyhow, and there she was.

Very still. Very peaceful.

And then she smiled. . . I suppose you could call it a smile. . . she smiled, and reached out her

136

frail arms toward me. . .

. . . and disappeared.

I was glad that it was over, for her sake, and glad that I'd been able to help her end it. But I was sad as well, because it was like losing a friend. I wonder what age she was, poor little thing?

I don't believe that I will ever see her again. I don't know whether I want to, or not. Seeing a ghost was exciting, probably the most exciting thing that will ever happen to me, but I am not a ghosty person, and once is enough!

I've still got the doll. I'm sure that Breige is right.

I'm sure my little ghost wanted me to have it.

A Selected List of Fiction from Mammoth

While every effort is made to keep prices low, it is sometimes necessary to increase prices at short notice. Mammoth Books reserves the right to show new retail prices on covers which may differ from those previously advertised in the text or elsewhere.

The prices shown below were correct at the time of going to press.

☐	416 13972 8	**Why the Whales Came**	Michael Morpurgo	£2.50
☐	7497 0034 3	**My Friend Walter**	Michael Morpurgo	£2.50
☐	7497 0035 1	**The Animals of Farthing Wood**	Colin Dann	£2.99
☐	7497 0136 6	**I Am David**	Anne Holm	£2.50
☐	7497 0139 0	**Snow Spider**	Jenny Nimmo	£2.50
☐	7497 0140 4	**Emlyn's Moon**	Jenny Nimmo	£2.25
☐	7497 0344 X	**The Haunting**	Margaret Mahy	£2.25
☐	416 96850 3	**Catalogue of the Universe**	Margaret Mahy	£1.95
☐	7497 0051 3	**My Friend Flicka**	Mary O'Hara	£2.99
☐	7497 0079 3	**Thunderhead**	Mary O'Hara	£2.99
☐	7497 0219 2	**Green Grass of Wyoming**	Mary O'Hara	£2.99
☐	416 13722 9	**Rival Games**	Michael Hardcastle	£1.99
☐	416 13212 X	**Mascot**	Michael Hardcastle	£1.99
☐	7497 0126 9	**Half a Team**	Michael Hardcastle	£1.99
☐	416 08812 0	**The Whipping Boy**	Sid Fleischman	£1.99
☐	7497 0033 5	**The Lives of Christopher Chant**	Diana Wynne-Jones	£2.50
☐	7497 0164 1	**A Visit to Folly Castle**	Nina Beachcroft	£2.25

All these books are available at your bookshop or newsagent, or can be ordered direct from the publisher. Just tick the titles you want and fill in the form below.

Mandarin Paperbacks, Cash Sales Department, PO Box 11, Falmouth, Cornwall TR10 9EN.

Please send cheque or postal order, no currency, for purchase price quoted and allow the following for postage and packing:

UK	80p for the first book, 20p for each additional book ordered to a maximum charge of £2.00.
BFPO	80p for the first book, 20p for each additional book.
Overseas including Eire	£1.50 for the first book, £1.00 for the second and 30p for each additional book thereafter.

NAME (Block letters) ....

ADDRESS ....

....

....